Travails of Faith

Travails of Faith

Alan J. Delotavo

FreshIdeasBooks
novel, candid, sensible

Travails of Faith

Cover design by Alan J. Delotavo. Cover photo credits acquired as royalty-free from dreamtimes.com: Exit ©Loke Yek Mang|Dreamstime.com; and Depression ©Aprescindere|Dreamstime.com

Published by FreshIdeasBooks, www.FreshIdeasBooks.com
ISBN: 978-0-9866306-9-9

For eBook and audio book versions and other books by Alan J. Delotavo see: www.delotavo.com

Dedication

*S*pecially written for *the open-minded Christians, the unchurched, the spiritual but not religious,* and *the secular*—who are seeking fresh meanings of "faith" amid the challenges in life!

Contents

Nuggets Of Christian Conundrum

ruth

hich of the varied forms of Christian faith is the truth? I bet everyone would say, "Mine!" Everyone presupposes their respective form of Christianity is *the* truth.

Everyone assumes their sets of doctrinal notions are directly handed over by God to them. Even the so-called liberal churches who seem to project an inclusive spirit are simply hiding, masquerading their deep conviction that their respective denominations hold the most truthful form of Christianity.

So, are all true? If so, there's nothing false. Are all false? If so, there's nothing true. Is only one form true? If so, God has become nothing but a sectarian idol favoring one and neglecting the rest. Are all saying varied aspects of the same truth? If so, they are all just clinging to varied fragments of truth. Then why not put these all together in a grand mosaic?

Or has the Christian faith, like many other religions, become a mere product of varied personal notions of differing theological entrepreneurs that have successfully marketed their conflicting theories into competing institutional systems of beliefs?

Can the essence of Christian truth still be recovered?

Faith

hat is faith?

Is it following a set of doctrines? Many do and regard themselves faithful. Is it an assumption resulting from an affirmation of God as having saved and reserved Heaven for Christian believers? Many assume so. Is it believing that one's church is the ark of salvation that offers the only refuge from the sins of the world? Also, many believe so.

Is it believing in Jesus as the only personal Savior? Most would agree. But what do we really mean by believing in Jesus? A mental affirmation? Of course, what else could an affirmation be but mental? How do we distinguish between a mental affirmation and a spiritual faith? Are these not all mental processes?

Or is faith more profound than what we usually assume it to be?

*L*ife

*W*hat, really, is the difference between Christian life and secular life? Or Christian life and the lives of other religious people? Or the lives of Christians belonging to varied churches?

A matter of lifestyle? But is the difference in lifestyle the bottom line for qualifying one to Heaven? Aren't these lifestyles merely cultural? Influenced by North American, European, African, Asian, or Latin American cultural carry-over to Christian practices?

Is morality confined to Christianity? Or is it a universal instinct expounded upon in a variety of theoretical frameworks, others in religious forms, some in secular concepts?

Is human life larger than religious beliefs? Or has religion, since the Medieval Era, tried to confine human life in the realm of religion? Is there profound happiness and fulfillment in life beyond denominational, or in a larger sense religious, prescriptions?

If human life is divine—reflective of the beauty and wonders of the Creator—aren't we also endowed with the creative potential to shape the fullness of life beyond the confines of religious biases and prejudices?

Marriage

*C*ould it be that the crumbling down of the ideals of a life-long marriage is already beyond the reach of the church? Because if it's within, renowned pastors and Christians who regularly attended church services could have been freed from the predicaments of divorce.

It seems faith in God couldn't transcend the propensity of marriages to break down. It seems that commitment to serve God couldn't prevent believers from engaging in premarital and extramarital sexual indulgences when they believed that sex outside marriage was unethical.

Usually, couples prefer church weddings over so-called civil unions. But do church blessings on marriage really endow blessings on the relationships between couples? Or is it simply a matter of momentary social prestige?

Is faith still a viable medium for preserving a lasting and happy marriage? If so, there would be no divorce among Christians.

Or have Christians, like others, already lost the essence of the sanctity and blessings of marriage, regarding it just like any other ordinary human relationship?

How, then, can we find hope for a lasting and happy marriage and family life?

Prayer

*P*rayer is one of the most misunderstood practices in Christianity.

In fact, it's the last thing a believer would let go of when leaving the church, because we all want to have somebody to lean on in case of need. We think that through prayer we've found the way to lean on the all-powerful God when we're in crisis situations. Or for others, when they ardently wish for something in life.

If prayer really works, why are all prayers not answered? If not all prayers are answered by God, then what prayers does He answer? I remember someone saying all prayers are answered by God. But is His answer yes, no, or wait? Is that God's answer, or simply one's ingenuity to find an answer to the enigma of prayer?

Does God still answer prayers today? If so, why doesn't He answer the plea for the healing of His beloved believers when they are gravely ill? Why can't we all, the more than one billion Christians in this world, join hands together to pray for God's miracles to save the hundreds of thousands of extremely malnourished and innocent children dying every day, and for an end to natural disasters? Or why don't we ask the so-called channels of God's divine healing to pray in every hospital so people can be healed and need hospitals, with their expensive bills, no more?

Or have Christians simply misunderstood the essence of prayer and what God intended it to be?

God's Will

What, really, is God's will?

Isn't it ludicrous and insane when someone who regards him or herself as the oracle of God declares, amid tragedies, that it's God's will for people, including innocent children, to suffer and die as punishment because they don't believe according to the oracle's notion of faith?

Oftentimes, we hear even pastors saying it's God's will for someone to die in a tragic accident or from incurable cancer. That's horrible. It's even more horrible to regard it as God's will that someone should annihilate others who believe otherwise. Sounds like a Muslim fundamentalist? No! Dig into history, and you'll see that Christians did that to who they regarded as pagans, and horribly did it also to one another in the name of conflicting beliefs about the same universal God they all worshipped.

Is it God's will that others become wealthy, like those on Forbes' list, and others be poor? So poor that the only place they can lie down at night is on a bedding of discarded cardboard on a cold and stinky street corner?

Does God plan for our respective careers in life? The person we marry and the children we raise? Or is everything in our own human hands with no divine intervention at all?

But could it also be that, indeed, there's such a thing as God's will—but we still have to unravel its profound meaning in our existence?

Divine Calling

*A*re each of us called by God to a particular vocation in life? If so, how can we know it? If not, is there such a thing, then, as being chosen by God? Many claim to be! But if God chooses only a handful of people to be His spokesmen or miracle healers, isn't this discriminating?

Ah! I know what those who claim to be chosen by God will say: it's God's choice. Really? Or is it just the direction in life they took, and luckily they became successful and feel good in claiming God's calling to preserve and advance their success, particularly those in church and para-church ministries? What about the secular people who also became globally successful, like the young billionaire tech gurus who don't go to church? Did God call them, too?

Is divine calling about one's career and job? Or is divine calling more profound and larger than what we usually think?

*L*ife

*L*ife! What does it mean? Is there a difference between life and existence? Do we live every day? Or do we simply exist every day? What does life in the Christian perspective mean? And what does life encompass?

Is there really a divine purpose for each of us? Or do we have to create our own divine purpose so we can live a purposeful life? Does God have a purpose for the lives of Christians? Of course, most Christians would affirm so. What about those who belong to other religions, like the Buddhists, Hindus, Muslims, and many others? Does God also have a purpose in their lives? What's the essential difference?

Is life merely human? Or do we belong to a larger system of universal life where all components need to be harmonious, from the tiniest atoms to the cosmological ecosystem, and to us? If human life is a lone entity, why do Christians envision a paradise of the new Heaven and new Earth? If human life belongs to a grand cosmological system, why don't Christians take good care of nature and the Earth?

Is life just a matter of waking up every day, preparing meals, going to work, coming back home, and doing the everyday routines? Is life just a mere perpetuation of mundane daily rituals until we become aged, die, and fade away?

Or is there more to life than what even Christians usually think of?

*P*rologue of the Travelogues

S piritual life has many phases. Just like our biological lives, where we grow and mature from infancy to adulthood, so in spiritual life we grow from new birth to struggles for meanings of faith to maturity. In each of these phases, beautiful memories are etched, full of depth, and these memories are what makes life beautiful.

The colors of struggle and survival, of frustrations and fulfillment, of meaninglessness and depths attained, indeed create a rainbow of life. Spiritual life is colorful, wonderful, and just beautiful. That's how amazing God's grace works.

Let me take you to the believers' journeys in search of meanings of faith. These were their adventures that carried their souls through rugged valleys, sharp edges, and steep climbs in life, ultimately ending in surprising discoveries. These were their exhilarating journeys! One of these could be like yours, too …

Where truth
is no longer meaningless

Truth is not merely about theological propositions;
truth is about the reality of ...

"**S**tunning!" Joel marveled at the beauty of an exotic hideaway. He could not help being amazed at the towering marble cliffs, enchanting lagoons, prehistoric caves, lush jungle, and mangrove forest dotted with refreshing waterfalls and alluring white sandy beaches.

"Perfect! No wonder CNNGo voted this as one of the best island destinations. At last, I've found a paradise." He sighed, exhaling the miasma of the stressful urban life while expecting that in El Nido he could finally find the answer to what he'd been seeking for quite some time.

Lying on a hammock tied between two coconut trees a-mid the ambience of a gentle sun and a cool breeze enlivening his weary body—a placid sea whispering quietly to his soul and a blue sky enthralling his mind to wander leisurely—he wondered ...

Is there really such a thing as the truth? If there's none, this implies that the world is lost. But the world is not chaotic without concepts of right and wrong, good and evil. The fact of orderly realities in the universe, the verity of morality, and the actuality of human life all indicate the existence of truth; otherwise, everything could just be illusory, false, and non-existing. Truth is about reality, and it's ridiculous to deny reality and the existence of truth.

But what about the truth about faith? If there is really such a thing as the true faith, which one is it among the numerous conflicting claims? The world is filled with all sorts of confusing claimants of truth—all asserting their respective notions as absolute.

My problem is not about the existence of God, but the truth of who He really is and what He really teaches. If I say only the Christian faith is the true faith, then which one is it a-mong the numerous conflicting theological, doctrinal, and denominational claims?

25

Why in the heck are there such things as Catholics, Protestants, Pentecostals, and independent churches—aside from the dizzying numbers of sub-groups within each church category—if there is only one God and one source of truth? Who says they are one or the other? Each has its own incompatible creed, doctrine, ritual, policy, bureaucracy, and other institutional matters. Are not these things simply tools to exploit believers and perpetuate one's exclusive brand of faith?

Each claimant, either church or prophet, theologian or believer, prides itself on its absolute divine origin—as if there's nothing else aside from it. Isn't this not only perplexing, but also deceiving? It appears that even the God of the universe could not help being confined to a particular notion that each one has formulated. In this sense, the personal God is merely transformed into an ideological god.

Each one is building a religious ideology after the other, and that ideology becomes not only the foundation of one's institutional identity, but also the very reason for which to die. Proponents of varied concepts of divine truth regard their theological theories as worth dying for. Is this sacrifice really worthy and sane? Or is it really nothing but a compulsive-obsessive delusion of securing an exclusive franchise of the afterlife? What about the warriors of truth: the inhuman murderers of others with differing views of God, who believe they were ordained by God Almighty to exterminate other humans God himself has created? I'm not just talking about Muslims and Christians killing each other, or Muslims among themselves, but also Christians annihilating one another. History proves that belief in the love of Jesus did not deter Christians from brutally murdering one another. Ludicrous insanity!

Even now, in the age of globalization, Christians still harbor antagonism against one another. They just can't give up their cold war and segregationist spirits, as if the Christ they all worship is powerless to join them together as one human family to model an ideal human race amid a broken world that longs for love and reunion.

There are even those who call themselves interdenominational or non-denominational fellowships who pop up every now and then, but they are essentially nothing more than superficial remakes of traditional segregated churches. I see these types of fellowships as religious enterprises to further complicate the already existing grave confusion in Christian faith.

But for what purpose? Further commercialization of the Christian faith? Obviously, I guess. But of course, like their predecessors, the already established churches of the Christian faith, they, too, want to have a share of the big pie. Just imagine the wealth of established churches, from real estate properties to large bank accounts that even surpass many multinational corporations, plus valuable relics worth millions, if not billions, of dollars.

No wonder most of the founders of mega-churches live extravagant lives, enjoying private jets, luxury vacation houses, pompous houses, glittering jewelry, and expensive toys. See how religious entrepreneurs become wealthy enjoying the luxuries of life, bilking their struggling middle-class members? Simple! Through a complicated system of exploiting and commercializing conscience.

Could not Christianity exist with just one set of beliefs and one church? Is there really a need for various conflicting claims? Could not Christian churches and leaders live modest lives and spend their money, say, building up a cooperative entrepreneurship for their church members to lift up their economic status?

But, well, whether I like it or not, the fact is, there are various and conflicting claims on the truth of Christian faith, and each church doggedly insists on preserving its own religious brands.

"Hah!" Joel sighed.

Why am I caught up in this mess of confusion when most Christians are at ease with their respective religious egos?

But I've got to know the truth, so I, too, can be certain of Heaven or know if Heaven, after all, is just an illusory philosophical creation ...

Caught in the mire of confusion of faith, Joel fell asleep in his soothing hammock.

A charming *mestiza*, half-Caucasian and half-Asian, awakened Joel with a gentle tap. "Excuse me. Sorry for waking you up."

Joel was surprised. "Nikki? Nikki!"

"Joel? Oh, dear! It's really you." Nikki's gut feeling had been right.

Nikki hugged Joel, who was still lying in the hammock. They hugged each other warmly and tightly, like long lost lovers.

"How's life?" Joel asked.

"Since we lost each other, I've tried to find ways to brighten my life. But oftentimes I thought of you. I knew you loved me. I'm sure we loved each other, but I don't know why we lost each other after graduation. My gut feeling said that somewhere unexpected I'd see you again," Nikki said.

"That sounds like a prophecy," Joel replied.

The romance between the two long-lost lovebirds was lit again, rekindling the love that had flickered ...

~

Fresh from his tropical getaway, Joel was enthused about life again. Not only did he have the break he'd wanted for some time, but he also again found the love he had been longing for since it began drifting.

But after a short while, the spiritual-philosophical-matter haunted him again. He was again preoccupied with seeking the truth about faith—the truth he believed could save him and ensure his future. He believed there was a truth, and he was even confident he could comprehend it.

"I have the capacity to know," he affirmed.

Intrigued by the enigma of the truth and driven by the desire to unravel it, he studied the Bible that had been lying dormant on his shelf for years. At the outset, his study was driven by curiosity; later, by a profound wish that he could discover something astounding that could revolutionize how Christians see faith.

"But where's the truth here amid all these stories and verses?" He was bewildered.

"I just can't understand this book," he lamented. He felt what multitudes of other seekers felt, too, when they first read the Bible.

His Bible study was even made dry by the odd English he couldn't understand. And worse, his study wasn't only boring, but also stressful. He was stressed from forcing himself to study a book he found no pleasure reading. He tried hastily praying before reading; perchance he'd have inspiration to study. But the narrations and sayings were boring him to death.

Then he got a spark of inspiration, an ingenuity, he assumed.

"Why not let the church teach me the truth? Yes! The church knows the truth! It can sift stories and messages for me, so what I get is just plain truth—convenient and quick! I don't have to go through the hassle of figuring out what the truth really is."

His search for Biblical truth led him to search for the true Church.

"But which church among several?" He was puzzled.

"Yeah! I got it. I should seek which among them is the original! There must be one; otherwise, Christianity is just nonsense filled with all sorts of confusions." He asked himself a question that had also confused many other seekers. "But could all of them be true churches also?"

So he put aside personal Bible study and ended up studying denominational doctrines instead, doctrines that he previously thought were nothing but eccentric exclusivist theories. He started window shopping among the nicest looking churches where respectable people attended, but soon realized that the differences among churches were not just doctrinal and institutional, but also ethnic and cultural.

"Now, how will I know which one teaches the truth?" he sighed, asking himself a profound question.

"Oh yes!" he quipped. "If I could clearly read their teachings in the Bible."

So he began the journey of shifting concepts.

One taught that Christ is not God. Without much ado, he reasoned, "If Jesus isn't God I don't want to be a Christian then. I would rather be a Taoist or a Confucian. Taoism and Confucianism have better environmental and social ethics than Christianity."

He found that other churches had sets of sacred writings other than the Bible. Again, without much ado, he pointed out, "This will just confuse me more." He thought those extra writings could take the place of the Bible as the standard book of faith.

While hopping from one church to another, he heard one preach, "Salvation is only through Christ Jesus!"

He concluded, "This is it! Now I've found the truth, just as easy as that!" He was so excited with this epiphany. He really thought he'd finally found the end of his journey.

Then he discovered that there were also several other churches preaching the same message, and he didn't expect that there were still other addenda to the simple statement

32

of "Salvation only through Christ Jesus!" Amid another batch of confusion, he almost gave up early in his search for truth. But, realizing he was already on first base and foreseeing a home run as still possible, he continued on his journey.

"Perhaps a few more hits, then I can have what I wish for." He took a chance.

Then he chose to attend one from among those who believed in Christ Jesus as God and as the only savior. After two weeks of attending evangelistic meetings in that church, an itinerant evangelist asked if he would accept Christ as his personal Savior. Without hesitation, he said, "Yes!" Although his assent didn't actually mean more than just a theoretical one. He was baptized and joined the church.

"Congratulations on your new life with Christ!" The pastor, a group of church leaders and some members greeted him.

"Welcome to your new home," a newfound friend said with a warm hug.

But he thought, "Will this really be my new home? Is this the end of my journey of faith? I just can't believe it. Is this what faith is all about?"

It didn't take him long to discover that his apprehension was right. A few weeks after the evangelist left, his excitement about church life began to wane until it finally dissipated.

The time came when attending church no longer appealed to him. His Bible readings became drier than when he'd first attempted to study, until he no longer read it. What lingered in his mind, though, were the stories of the Bible that caught his curiosity. He wondered what those stories really meant. Finally, his enthusiasm for attending church services faded away. He was counted as one of the victims of fleeting evangelism without sensible long-term pastoral care.

Being born in a so-called "Christian" country, his belief in the existence of God was rooted in his psyche, but the meanings and implications of that belief in his everyday life were still enigmatic.

After years of not attending church anymore, he unexpectedly met his beloved high school teacher. She was already long retired but still beaming with enthusiasm for teaching. She also exhibited that same kind and cheerful spirit. Meeting her reminded Joel a bit of his wild high school days. They chuckled, sharing their memories. His teacher asked for his phone number, and afterwards she gave Joel a buzz almost every weekend, wooing him to attend church.

To please her after almost a year of persistently buzzing him, Joel finally consented. He also attended a Bible study before the main service started. To ease his boredom, he posed knotty questions to the Bible study leader, who often-times couldn't answer his inquiries. Joel could sense how uneasy the study leader was every time he attended the session.

Joel wasn't really spiritually serious about the Bible study. He regarded it as an avenue to let off the steam of his intellectual frustrations over the meaninglessness of faith that confronted him. As soon as the church service started, the lullaby hymns were like depressants that made him drowsy. The sermons, too, made no sense to him. How he wished the service would end quickly.

But one day, while reading the teachings of his teacher's church, he came across a doctrine he thought unique from the rest. He doublechecked the Bible passages, and indeed, there he found it. He thought all other churches simply ignored the clear and simple truth he had found. The impression became deeper until he was persuaded to join his teacher-friend's church.

"At last, this is the true church I've been searching for!" he affirmed.

He was baptized again—for the third time, actually: two immersions when he was an adult, and one sprinkling when he was a baby. He joked, "If baptismal rite guarantees Heaven, I could be one of the most assured living saints." He expected that his second adult baptism would finally be the highlight of his new birth experience. He didn't expect more poignant ones were coming that would haunt him for the rest of his life.

After baptism, a divine calling germinated in his heart. He felt God was prompting him to serve as a pastor-theologian, so he shifted careers and forsook the one he had cherished since childhood. His career shift surprised his family and friends, who were either occasionally attending church or not attending at all. They couldn't understand why.

Theology became his new world, and converting people to God's kingdom became his new career cliché. He was determined to dedicate his whole life to the service of God.

"Could there be a nobler career on Earth than assuring people's salvation in Heaven?" he said to himself with a great sense of pride over his newfound career.

"Outside the church, there is no salvation," he preached with deep conviction. "Outside the church, there's no other truth," he affirmed. And by 'the church,' he meant only his particular church. He taught his church's doctrine as the only gospel and passionately defended it as the only truth.

Then his passion for theology led him to further schooling. Confident that he held the only truth, he decided to

36

study in an interdenominational theological school, hoping to share the truth he'd discovered with others.

One day, he attended an inter-church theological forum, joined by pastors from various churches. He was enthused that in this forum he could share his faith and lead others in his church. "I'm going to lead them to Jesus. I'm going to lead them to the only true church Christ has established on Earth," he said zealously.

"Salvation by faith alone!" one declared.

"Not by faith alone, but by God's grace alone!" another refuted.

"Neither by faith, nor by grace alone, but by God's grace through faith!" someone synthesized.

"But what faith? Imputed or imparted?" another asked.

"It doesn't matter as long as it is faith that works, living faith at that. In fact, that faith should lead us to work for the welfare of the poor rather than merely relax on the pews as if watching holy shows," a follower of social gospel pointed out.

"No! It matters. It should be a faith that results in obedience," a legalist asserted.

"Obey what?" somebody asked.

"The Ten Commandments, of course. Both literally and spiritually," the legalist answered back.

"That's legalism!" a liberal pastor criticized.

"But even faith itself is a divine gift. So is grace, of course. And what if you reject grace—will your faith save you?" a conservative pastor asked.

"No, of course not, but without the hand of faith, grace can't be received either. That's what the Bible plainly says," a fundamentalist emphasized.

"You cannot know the truth by just reading the Bible plainly; that's too literal. You've got to decipher the messages beyond the literal words that were written thousands of years ago in a totally different cultural context than the present," another liberal minded pastor argued.

"That's absurd! Every word written in the Bible is inspired by God. The Bible came from God, word for word," another fundamentalist pastor defended.

"That's problematic, though. For what about matters like not allowing women to speak in church? Or imposing rituals on women on their monthly period?" a feminist pastor retorted.

"That's why we don't ordain women," the fundamentalist pastor replied.

"And that's where you're wrong! You're still clinging to an uncivilized form of male-dominated religion," the feminist responded.

"That's why Karl Barth said—" another one attempted to explain his point.

"No! Read Emil Brunner's writing, and you'll find that Karl Barth was wrong," someone interrupted.

"Why don't we just come back to what the Bible teaches?" a confused pastor blurted.

"You're too fundamentalist," accused one.

"That's better than being a liberal who treats the Bible as secular literature," defended another.

"What's with all these arguments?" a latecomer asked Joel.

"I don't know! I don't know what the heck they're doing ..." Joel replied, overwhelmed by confusion and losing grip on his personal witnessing purposes.

The latecomer pastor reacted with disgust. "Wow! Certainly, the Bible shouldn't be treated as secular literature. It should be regarded as holy, but why all these dogged contentions and confusions?"

Burdened and bothered, Joel left the forum hall and retreated to his bachelor's quarters. Sitting on the lounge chair while staring into the sky, he remembered the hideaway he'd taken years back. Then he wondered again...

Why are those guys certain of what they thought, despite their intellectual limitations? Isn't God larger than any and all of their thoughts? If that's how they treat doctrine, then doctrine is not all there is in truth, nor all there is in Christian faith.

There must be something more profound in faith and truth about God than mere concepts and beliefs.

If doctrine is sacred, it could have not divided and confused Christians, but instead united them as one loving family of Christ. Has doctrine become a prop to preserve and promote one's denominational institutional agenda? Now I'm beginning to realize that Christian faith has merely become a matter of doctrinal concept. Having varied doctrinal concepts is not the key to salvation. In fact, it even destroys faith.

And I don't believe either that God is preoccupied with judging who among his worshippers has the best doctrinal theory about Him. I believe what God is looking for among His followers is something more sensible and more life-transforming than mere conflicting theological expositions. He's not merely someone who sits on His throne, waiting for someone to deliver the best speech about Him, as if it's a sort of Toastmasters' after-dinner speech.

Theological concepts merely shape one's biases and prejudices and cannot save humanity and ensure humanity's future. Only the universal God can. Doctrinal contentions, no matter how scholarly they seem to be, just can't fulfill the deepest yearnings of believers struggling for meaningful faith amid their struggles in everyday life.

Besides, what's really theological scholarship? Just a new way of retelling what has been previously said in contrast to what others have also said? If a non-Christian searches for meanings of faith, will he be interested in becoming a Christian if all he gets is a variety of conflicting doctrinal arguments to choose from? But why are Christian churches preoccupied with conflicting doctrines? And why the preoccupation with something that causes division and confusion?

And if all doctrines are true, why are they different from one another? If they are all aspects of one bigger truth, why are these divisive instead of unifying? And if there is only one true doctrine, whose is it? I think everybody would doggedly claim, "Mine!" but if everything is true, then there can't really be a false doctrine. If everything is false, then there can't really be the true one.

I came here to share what I believed is the truth; now I'm confused even more. I came here to enrich and share my faith; now I'm beginning to question the veracity of what I believe. Now I don't know what to do. I don't know what to believe anymore.

Bewildered, the following day he went to the library and did some reading; however, the more stressed he became reading theology books replete with words he couldn't understand written by famous theologians praised as scholarly, the more they defied common understanding. After a couple hours in the library, he rushed to his apartment, closed the door, and screamed, "Ahhh! I left my well-paying career to dedicate my life to God, and what have I here? A petty job propagating a particular theory of faith? Ahhh!"

He'd expected that in a reputable theological school, he would take an inspiring journey of faith, but he'd ended up on the verge of losing faith. Taking a chance that a different learning context would answer his spiritual needs, he pursued another graduate study in the interdisciplinary religious department of the same university.

A deeper understanding of human nature, culture, and society will probably help me enrich my faith and become a more sensible pastor-theologian, he thought.

So he took an interdisciplinary study focusing on religion, culture, and psychology. He studied psychology of religion but ended up regarding spirituality as a mere psychological experience. He studied sociology of religion but ended up regarding religion as a mere social phenomenon. He studied cultural anthropology and religion but ended up regarding humans as mere higher forms of animal species filled with wonder but devoid of divine mystery.

"Where's God and faith now? Is this all that human existence and life is? What about hope in the future? Do I have hope for my personal future? Is there hope for the human race? What shall I do with my faith now, more so of my career?" he pondered.

42

Not wanting to give up his quest for truth, he resorted to a more down-to-Earth approach to Christian faith and ministry: social gospel. "After all," he said, "Christ loved the poor, and in fact, he came to save them."

Gospel for the poor, justice, equality, social transformation, and struggles for liberation became his new career clichés. He regarded social gospel as real, practical, and something that really touched the lives of people.

He then joined an international para-church organization ministering to the oppressed and the deprived people in Asia and Africa. His soul was deeply touched seeing the sufferings of many people, and in one way or another helped alleviate it. It was there he found another aspect of his faith—compassion!

But one night after a tough day of seeing a number of deaths, including extremely malnourished children, very sick mothers still holding their dying babies in their arms, and dying fathers who were victims of ethnic cleansing hopelessly staring at their afflicted helpless families, he grew overwhelmed by the unimaginable suffering. He shivered sitting on his bunkbed, stricken with grave anxiety and fear like never before. "Oh God, oh God ...," he uttered while shivering 'til his last drop of energy was drained. Then he slumped into the bed, falling like he was dead.

He woke up late the following morning and decided to go home. Before leaving the humanitarian camp, he earnestly poured out his burden to God, praying, "Jesus, I don't know what to do. I'm afraid of life. I'm struggling for meaning in my faith. I don't know where I'm going. Show me the way. Show me the truth about human life and existence. The truth about you. The truth about how I can find peace and fulfillment in life. Please ..."

~

Not finding the truth he was seeking, he slowly drifted into the world again. He lost his zeal for pastoral ministry, sought a secular job, and began enjoying what Christians would call the "pleasures of the world," where he found solace.

But he also enjoyed greater financial stability than before and decided to build a new countryhouse on the outskirts of the city, where he thought he could find more peace. He dated young women one after the other, seeking love, despite the fact that Nikki still lingered in his heart. But his previous journey of faith had taken him to foreign lands where he'd lost track of her again.

Then, one night, he felt the urge to call 911 before it was too late. He felt strangely sick. He lived a healthy life before.

But after leaving the pastoral service, his habit of eating unhealthy fast foods, alcohol, sedentary life, and lack of good sleep almost every night threatened his health. When the ambulance arrived, he was rushed to the hospital and found himself clinging on to life.

Alone and dreadfully fearing the loss of his life in an intensive care unit, he remembered the Jesus he'd left years ago and cried for help. "Lord, please save me. I know I have drifted, but you know my heart. You know my struggles in life. Deep within me, I still believe in you. I was seeking for you, but I got lost. Please give me another chance, and please help me find what the truth about faith really is."

"Joel," an uplifting and assuring voice whispered, "more than the love any human could give is the love of God. He still loves you, Joel. He still loves you."

As Joel wiped his tears and began to see clearly, he saw a very familiar figure. Her gentle voice and lovely touch was like a balm that gradually healed Joel's heart. Joel, unable to speak yet, just stared at her feeling sorry that he hadn't given much care to her and the love she'd had for him. Tears trickled down Joel's face. Glancing at all the tubes attached to his body after open heart surgery, the fear of life engulfed him more than the fear he'd felt years back on the night before he left the humanitarian camp in Africa.

45

"Have faith, Joel. You've got to believe that God is able to heal you and give you your life back again. I love you, and I always will." Nikki tenderly kissed Joel's forehead, then quietly left the room.

Feeling so feeble and hopeless, he could not help calling on the God he oftentimes forgot. He poured out all his anxieties, his heart's desires, frustrations about the Christian faith, the uncertainty of his future, and even regrets for neglecting the love he and Nikki had once promised to cherish 'til death. Now, fearful he may no longer have time to live and enjoy the love that was once so beautiful, he sobbed like a helpless baby, begging for help from the father he was doubtful was still there.

"Believe ..." Nikki's words reverberated in his soul. "I believe in you, Jesus." And he slept.

~

A couple weeks passed, and he realized Jesus was saving him from the brink of death, giving him the opportunity to live again and live a new life. Right on his hospital bed, he experienced a new birth more poignant and profound than the conversion he'd had before when he was merely seeking concepts of truth.

Then he realized what it meant to be transformed from glory to glory while still on Earth. Being already able to rise a bit from the bed and lean on the headboard, he took a Kindle Bible in New Living Translation from the side table and read it. This time, he was no longer figuring out concepts, but rather listening to Jesus telling him life-transforming stories.

He searched for truth in the realms of doctrinal theories and found meaninglessness of faith. He encountered Jesus at an unexpected place in unexpected moments, and he found meaning in life.

He discovered what the truth in Christian faith really was: not merely theological propositions; truth is about the reality of relationships, trust, and everyday experiences in life as the result of faith in Jesus.

Joel discovered what Jesus meant when he said, "I am the Way, the Truth, and the Life." In Jesus, Joel found rest from the restlessness of his soul, and while his body was healing, his life was also transforming into something truly new.

"There must be a grand purpose for all these happenings in my life …" he beamed, foreseeing a more fulfilling future as his fresh life of faith was unfolding. He was enthused that this time his life was no longer lonely and dull, but beautifully colored by the love of his Heavenly Father and the love of the lady he had cherished for so long.

Where faith
is no longer confusing

*Faith is not merely about learning
what religion teaches. It's about having a deep ...*

"*I* think you'll find the answer in Asia!" TJ joked.

"Interestingly, I have a gut feeling that indeed I will!" Shari replied.

"And what makes you think so?" TJ asked.

"Because most of us think civilization began in the Middle East because it's near to what we Christians call the Holy Land, and in particular it describes where the Garden of Eden was. Now we know that there's not one, but multiple cradles of civilizations, and most of those were in Asia," Shari replied.

48

"So you mean Christians manipulated the academic world into believing the location of the Garden of Eden was the only cradle of civilization?" TJ asked.

"Indeed! That tradition of monopolizing the academe started in Constantinople in 325 A.D., when Constantine wanted to have only one set of Christian beliefs. Then, from the Roman Empire and the so-called western countries that came from it, the control and institutionalization of western knowledge was perpetuated. Even today, we still think that the only standard of knowledge is western knowledge, even though many of our North American and western European universities are now rated below a number of Asian universities," Shari pointed out.

"Well, here you are again. You're a purebred North American, but you speak like an Asian activist," TJ commented.

"No, it's not about that," Shari emphasized. It's about knowing what the truth really is. If knowledge has been controlled since the Middle Ages, particularly by the church, how do we know that the Christian faith is indeed true? And at the outset, how do we know the truth about the Christian faith? Or if it's the only truth about God?"

TJ drew near to Shari and sweetly hugged and kissed her. "Oh, c'mon, my dear Shari. Let's just go to Asia, relax, and enjoy the exotic wonders of the Orient. Promise me we'll have fun on our trip instead of arguing about mystical things. At times, it gets boring, you know. Let's just have a life. Let's just have fun. Deal, my dear?"

"Deal, my dear," she answered. "As long as you don't forget that I missed our bedtime talks," she added.

"Sure, as long as you don't forget it's our anniversary getaway, Hon," TJ replied, smiling.

TJ carefully planned the trip and saw to it that in every place they visited, they'd be staying in a cozy cabin, a classy Oriental hut, an elegant beach house, or a lodge amid nature, which was more exotic and a break from the humdrum of the usual urban North American hotels. He also made sure that he and Shari both got what they were wishing for. He wanted to see nature, and Shari wanted to see ancient shrines, particularly mysterious ones. The more mysterious the shrine, the more it excited her.

~

"Holy!" Shari exclaimed. "Those diamonds, gold, and rubies worth millions of bucks are just laying open in public and never stolen? Unbelievable! Do that in Central Park and it wouldn't last for a night or two."

"Or even a few hours," TJ said jokingly.

Shari was awed, staring at the grandeur of the Shwedagon Pagoda in Myanmar, which was covered in sparkling

50

gold, a mesmerizing 2,000 rubies, and a glittering 5,000 diamonds, including a 76 carat at the Pagoda's tip. The eight strands of what's believed to be Buddha's hair amused her, though.

"Look, TJ, do you really believe it's Buddha's hair?" Shari asked.

"Shh, that's sacrilege," TJ replied. "This relic is sacred for Buddha's devotees. Imagine having strands of hair of Jesus in Westminster Abbey."

The couple continued their exotic anniversary adventure in the Alaungdaw Kathapa National Park. It was both a natural park and a religious site where about 30,000 pilgrims a year paid homage to sacred animals, particularly wild pigs and tigers. TJ was awed seeing animals he'd never seen before, like large herds of Asian elephants, sun bears, giant squirrels, barking deer, and various types of birds.

"This is truly a paradise!" TJ exclaimed.

After Myanmar, the couple flew to India and went to see the Gudimallam Shiva Temple, believed to be the oldest Hindu temple with the oldest sacred relic .

Shari laughed. "What?! The most ancient holy relic of a Hindu god is a phallus?"

"Shari, stop. People are staring at you," TJ said.

"Sorry, I can't, but ..." Shari continued laughing, amused by what she saw.

"C'mon, let's take a break outside and come back when you're in a more somber mood. You're offending these people." TJ gently grabbed Shari's arm while they slowly walked out.

Once outside, the more Shari laughed, so did TJ. "Imagine you're married to a devotee of this shrine. Your phallus could have been used as a model for a family altar," Shari said, guffawing. So did TJ.

After their silliness dissipated, they joined the small group with the tour guide explaining that the relic portrayed the Hindu Trinity Brahma, Vishnu, and Shiva. While touring around, the sense of mystery that lingered throughout their getaway seeped into Shari's soul.

Then the lovebirds, whose romance had flared again, took off for an unusual trip to China, to the world's foremost Taoist temple of the White Cloud. There, Shari was mesmerized by the mystical serenity of the relics and the ambience. Caught up in a strange feeling of oneness with the universe, she sat down in a corner of a bridge, wondering about that real things that bridge humans with the larger reality of life and universal existence.

"The Way. What's the way all about?" she reflected.

"Hon', time to move on," TJ said after finding her.

They continued their Beijing trip to the Fragrant Hills Park. There, they both found an atypical release from the hustle and bustle of life. From the spectacular scenery of red-smoke tree leaves blanketing the mountains, to the water parks embodying both the serenity of the pond and the liveliness of the fountain and the artful falls, and the landscape captivating the balance of nature and human-made structures, they were like spas that soothed their weary souls.

TJ was awed. "Dear, this is a Shangri-La."

"See what life could be like if we humans would just live a balanced, natural life," Shari said to TJ while both were staring at a pond. "It's so invigorating. You feel as if your life flows from and with nature. It's so natural. It's so alive. It's not like living the mechanical life we've made for ourselves, being engrossed in the selfish preoccupation of artificial reality. "

"Yes, Hon, I feel it. It's as if a divine energy is being infused into our bodies and souls. I've never felt life like this before," TJ replied.

"This is not just something artificially spiritual," Shari replied, "this is profoundly spiritual, while also deeply physical."

"Wow! This is the most astonishing part of our adventure so far. Could there be more surprises?" TJ asked.

"Hmm, I have a gut feeling that something even grander will unfold," Shari replied.

From Beijing, the couple went to see the Temple of Confucius in Qufu. It was the largest and most famous Confucian temple, and also an UNESCO World Heritage Site.

Upon entering the temple, Shari instantly felt the ambience of an exotic royalty. Not the kind of pompous royalty that displays glittering crowns, jewels, and regalia, but a deeper feeling of royalty budding from a sense of noble, reciprocal community life.

"Harmony with nature, harmony with one another—aren't these the essences of human life?" Shari said.

"Now it seems that I'm indeed finding the answer to the meaning of life I've been seeking for a long time," she added with mixed feelings. A feeling of surprise that finally she'd found the answer she was seeking came over her, mixed with a feeling of anticipation that somehow there must still be something more beyond.

"Well, Hon, China is beautiful. But let's see what Japan has to offer," TJ said.

They flew from China to Japan. TJ and Shari were curious of what the Shinto shrine of Ujigami looked like and what spiritual discoveries and natural wonders awaited them there. They supposed that, being the oldest Shinto shrine in Japan and also a UNESCO World Heritage Site, something surprising awaited them there, too.

"Are we going to have a demo of a samurai there? Or probably learn a bit of ninja?" Shari joked, as if her reflective mood was transcended by her usual buoyant and carefree spirit.

They joined a small group of westerners touring the site. A Japanese tour guide who spoke good English with a Japanese accent told them the story behind the shrine. Upon hearing the tragic story of imperial succession and imagining the brutality of being killed by a sword, an eerie feeling of the ghosts of beheaded people wandering around beset her.

"TJ, I don't feel like going further. Can we just go to our cabin?" Shari said.

"Why? Something wrong?" TJ asked.

"I feel spooky here," Shari replied.

"You must be imagining something. I'm tired anyway, so let's go then," TJ said.

While TJ was taking a shower, Shari went to relax on a wicker lounging chair on their cabin's balcony, overlooking a beautiful and serene Zen garden. The moon was full, the glittering stars adorned the sky, and the gentle sound of crickets filled the air amid the gentle breeze. Staring into the distance, scenes of the shrines flashed back in her mind, then she began reflecting ...

What does it really mean to believe in Jesus? At the outset, why did I believe in Christianity instead of other religions? Or why did I believe just in Christianity and not in some or all of the other religions also? Why am I not a Hindu, a Buddhist, a Taoist, a Confucian, a Shinto, or a Muslim? Am I a Christian simply because I was born in a Christian-believing society? What if I was born in a Hindu country—would I still be a Christian?

Did God destine me to be a Christian while He destined the rest of the billions of people in this world to be non-Christians? That would be very discriminatory if salvation is only through Christianity. It means that He destined billions of innocent people—who are also his precious human creatures—to be lost to Heaven.

Most Christians would say that's why we need to evangelize and convert the whole world into Christianity, but it's a ridiculous proposition. In the first place, Christians could never convert the whole world to the Christian faith. In the second place, it would make Christianity—which is just one of the three western religions, the exclusive franchisee of Heaven— despite the fact that there are also numerous conflicting forms of Christianity.

56

I must convince myself of why I am a Christian and not a follower of other religions. Perhaps I'm just socially conditioned to become a Christian. But aren't all religions also good? Do they not all have the same purpose?

The very relaxing ambience of the night lulled Shari into a deep sleep while reflecting upon her faith.

~

A week after their anniversary getaway, Shari began searching for answers about faith. She studied the beliefs of different religions, trying to understand their respective ultimate goals. She felt that if she could just unravel the goal of each religion, it would make sense to her whether she would continue to be a Christian or not, or even become a hybrid believer.

She attended a class in World Religion under a respected scholar, but after a couple weeks dropped out. Each class session bored her to catnap.

"What the heck is he saying? I just want to know what each religion teaches about human life and how we can achieve fulfillment in our everyday lives—in plain and clear English. This guy is talking alien."

So she decided to do it the handy way: online research. Bingo! She began getting what she wanted. She learned that

57

Hinduism teaches *Moksha*, or deliverance from the cycle of rebirth in the world. When that is attained, there will be no more existence in this world.

"An existence in nothingness?" She was puzzled. "So the purpose of Hinduism is to deny the material world and look forward to non-existence? That's a life too abstract to be meaningful to me," she concluded.

She studied Buddhism and learned about *Nirvana*, a state of enlightenment, and an existence of self in the realm of mystical consciousness.

"Enlightenment sounds interesting, but *Nirvana* is just another version of *Moksha*. One is an unconscious state, the other is conscious. But these are all simply a state of mind, and if the goal of human life is mystical enlightenment and non-materialistic life, why all the glitter of gold, diamonds, and rubies in the shrines? And why does the Hindu temple portray eroticism when the goal is otherworldly? That's contradictory.

"*Nirvan*a is as abstract as *Moksha*, and although the enlightenment part of *Nirvana* is more attainable than *Moksha*, both Buddhism and Hinduism still regard everyday life and existence as illusory. Life on Earth is beset by many problems; that's why I'm searching for sensible ways of coping with life, not a way to escape reality. And what is *Nirvana* anyway? I bet it's just a mental state or a type of perception." She concluded, "No, I still want to have a more sensible and realistic form of religion. No, these are not for me.

"What about Confucianism? It teaches an ethical way of life through mutual respect and reciprocation. That's great! If people would just live humanely with one another, the world would be a great place to live. There would be a more equitable society. Business dealings would be less fraudulent. Politicians would be focused on meeting the needs of the people rather than fulfilling corporate lust. And our society would be more humanizing. This is just a great social teaching. Yeah! These are the values that transformed Singapore from an insignificant marsh to a progressive and cleaner society, both physically and politically. Wow! I should take serious note of this.

"But aside from social ethics, what about hope in the hereafter? Where am I going when I'm on the brink of reaching the limit of my life? What about times I'm helpless and groping in the dark for a supernatural source of hope?

"What about hope in the future of planet Earth? What if a huge meteor strikes the Earth? God forbid! Or if the world were devastated by global warming?

"I need somebody much bigger than death and destruction to give me hope in the future. Or at least more profound than the fear of death and destruction to give me a sense of direction in life.

She concluded: "Social ethics is good, and I would regard this as part of a short list of answers, but there must be something more than this."

"What about Taoism?" she reflected.

"It teaches harmony with nature, like harmony in society; harmony with nature is important to life on Earth. If humans lived in harmony with the whole system of nature, global warming wouldn't haunt us today. Life could have been ..." Then she remembered the feeling of living in paradise—like the Shangri-la ambience when she and TJ had visited the Fragrant Hills Park.

"Yeah, it could have been like that. Was that a foretaste of what life could be if humans regenerated nature and lived a balanced life?

"Wow!" she said, imagining her delight in living in the ideals of the harmonious system of human and natural life.

"So now, what's my alternative to the Christian faith? And how does the Christian faith compare to these Oriental religions?" she asked herself.

"But wait a minute, what about the so-called western religions? Okay, let me take a look at them first before finally making a more rational decision on whether or not I still wish to be a Christian because I found it more sensible than the rest. Maybe I'll even devise a hybrid form of faith." She was enthusiastic in her quest.

She researched Islam and Judaism and no essential difference between Islam and Judaism except cultural overtones. Both believed in one God, Allah in Islam and Yahweh in Judaism. Both emerged from a political-military background, one from a context of establishing its statehood, the other of converting other territories into its faith.

And both shared similar sacred stories, but geared to their respective vindication as the only true faith. And Islam, like Christianity, was preoccupied with vindicating itself as the only true faith and conquering others, while Judaism concerned itself in perpetuating its ethnocentric faith. So, while the conflict between Jews and Muslims was always political, the conflict between Muslims and Christians was always religious.

She also discovered that Islam was closer to Judaism than Christianity was to Judaism. She also found out that, contrary to the current popular notion, Christians persecuted both Jews and Muslims, while there was even a time when Jews and Muslims had lived harmoniously together.

She also learned that both Judaism and Islam taught about life in the hereafter. Judaism wished for a literal Jewish kingdom that would rule the world, while Islam for a more mundane Heaven filled with the finest wines and beautiful virgins. Christianity, on the other hand, wished for a more somber, idealized form of Earthly life.

"Now, what shall I be?" She sighed, confused about what to believe and what not to believe.

"I'm beginning to realize that there's really no difference between theistic religions. It seems I'm beginning to find more sense in non-theistic oriental religions like Taoism and Confucianism and some aspects of Buddhism. Does this mean I have to give up my Christian faith for Oriental religion?"

She had been searching for a belief system that could make a difference in her everyday life, but faced with the anxiety of embracing a foreign faith and giving up her traditional Christian faith, she let go of her concerns about faith.

For the moment, she concluded: "Yeah, life will go on. I don't really need to be that faithful. It will just make my life more complicated. I think TJ is right. I just need to enjoy life and lay aside those extramundane concerns. What's important is that I'm happy with what life offers me every day as a normal human being. I really don't need to be a saint or a monk to find happiness in this world. Happiness is just around the corner every day."

~

Then one day, while driving home after a community meeting aimed at developing a cooperative entrepreneurship for the poor, her SUV was struck by a pickup truck driven by a drunk driver. She lost consciousness immediately upon impact. A witness to the accident immediately called 911, and she was rushed to the hospital in a coma.

While in a coma, she gained consciousness of a different level of existence. Some might call it a deep dream world, but in her dream she believed she had been taken to Heaven.

"Where am I?" she asked a shadowy figure amid the most pleasing light she had ever seen.

"You're in another dimension of life and existence. See those ...?" The angelic figure pointed to what looked like a hologram of everyday life on Earth.

"That's my husband, and those are my friends and people I loved," Shari said in surprise.

"Look what they're doing," the angel said.

"Looks like they're just living a normal everyday life. And they all look fine and happy," Shari said.

"But look what happens next," the angel said.

"Whoa! Oh no! Not that!" she exclaimed, seeing the secret, appalling things they did, the tragedies that happened, and the wrong decisions they made in life. "Are they all going to be miserable afterward? Hopeless and broken? With no hope in life? And how did I get here?"

"Look!" the angel said, pointing to the last scene of her life.

"But that's unfair! That drunk guy hit my car? You mean I'm dead?" Fear engulfed her like never before. "But if I'm dead, why am I ... what? Am I in Heaven?"

"That's not important for now. What's important is you watch." The angel pointed to another holographic scene of life on Earth.

She sought for an answer. "They're all miserable! While enjoying life on Earth, suddenly life changed and they're all miserable? Is that what life is all about? A fleeting moment of joy, then suddenly misery and tragedy?"

"Yes, life on Earth is very uncertain. Yes, you're right, it's so fleeting. See all those artificial things those people, including your husband and friends, have heaped up? Those are really nothing. These are vain acquisitions. Look at their faces at the last moments of their lives; what do you see?"

"Ohhh!" She sighed with a heavily troubled heart while tears were trickling down her cheeks as she sobbed.

"Yes," the angel said, "the loneliness of leaving loved ones and friends, empty looks of uncertainty, fear of death slowly lurking, and—"

She couldn't bear to see the vanity of life on Earth. She grieved deeply.

"But that's not the end of the story. That is what could happen if not for this very important thing. Look there!" The angel pointed to another scene. "What do you see?"

"They're not sad. They're not miserable, nor hopeless. They're beaming with hope, as if they're facing tragedies in life with courage and peace," Shari said, awed.

"That's what you call faith, Shari. And look who's holding their hands, healing their souls, whispering hope to them ..." the angel said.

"What?" Shari was astounded. "Is that Jesus?" she asked.

"Yes! You see, if you believe in a personal God, the God who knows your needs, the God who became human so He could restore human life and existence back to something divine, you'll have hope. You'll have the courage to face the realities of life. You'll have a deep anchor for your soul. Go tell Him, talk to Him, and make Him a part of your everyday life ..." the angel said in the sweetest voice that had ever reverberated in Shari's soul. That voice and the scene infused in Shari a healing spirit.

~

After a couple weeks in the hospital, Shari woke up. After a couple months of rehab, she was able to recover like nothing had happened at all.

During the launching of a faith-based cooperative entrepreneurship which she envisioned would uplift the poor, both physically and spiritually, she testified to a stadium packed with people: "Let me share with you what I discovered about faith. It's not merely about learning what one religion after another teaches. It's about having a deep anchor in your soul. It's about having the courage and the serenity to live life every day while enjoying God's blessings—because we have faith that God, through Jesus, truly cares for us and our future."

Where life
is no longer broken

*The essence of Christian life is not
merely about living up to the expectations
of the church. It's about the daily ...*

"Now we're in Sziget. I can't believe we finally made it to the best of the European major festivals," said a jubilant fellow tourist while tapping Frankie's shoulders." I can't wait to hear all sorts of music: rock, pop, hip hop, electronic, everything. I didn't expect there could also be a plethora of activities here, from rock climbing to bungee jumping, life-size football, and many more. Oh! And did I forget to say a lot of dazzling ladies, too? This is going to be the best week of my life ever! A week of rockin', man ..."

"Here comes another nuisance," Frankie said to himself. But as he thought it, he realized the guy seemed familiar.

After checking into his hotel, Frankie went around to see the leaf village. When evening came, while everybody else was beginning to enjoy the buzz of music, booze, and the company of women, he was alone in his suite. He couldn't understand why he'd come to enjoy the buzz of the Sziget Festival but wanted to stay like a monk meditating amid revelry.

He reminisced on his rollercoaster life. He remembered about six years ago, he had been a faithful Christian and his life had seemed divine. But after discovering the hidden lives and immorality of a number of church leaders, he'd begun to lose his faith. At first, he thought corruption in the church was just a rare occasion; later, he discovered many other skeletons in the church's closet.

He was upset that the corruption in the world also happened inside the church, in even more deceptive ways. He struggled with this revelation for some time, until finally realizing there was really no difference between the supposedly holy church and the supposedly secular world. Both were just human worlds where beliefs were nothing but a facade in the pursuit of selfish ends—money and power. He also realized that, after all, secular people were even less pretentious than Christians, more so of church bureaucracy.

So he left the church.

Deep in his heart, the conviction of being faithful to God still haunted him, yet he felt that finding God inside the church was no better than finding Him outside. At times, he would like to live like people with no God—free to do what's pleasurable. But oftentimes his conscience would bother him as if a deep-seated voice was directing him somewhere and he still didn't know where.

He reflected ...

What really is the meaning of Christian life? I was once a Christian because I accepted my church's teachings as true, followed my church's dos and don'ts, regularly attended church services, read the Bible, and prayed to God.

Yes, Christianity was my way of life, but being just one of the many lifestyle alternatives, it's even more undesirable because it's hypocritically used to deceive people into thinking that Christians are holier than others.

Besides, Christianity is not the only religion in the world. There are still other people who believe in the sacredness of their teachings and the truthfulness of their God. I call their object of worship 'God' because don't all religions worship one God beyond superficial religious differences? And isn't the difference between Christianity and other religions merely a matter of superficial cultural forms? Christianity in a more Western cultural form, and others in a more Oriental or Middle Eastern cultural form?

And by the way, what really is sin? Most Christians believe in monogamy, while others accept polygamy. Hinduism even has the *Kama Sutra*, which portrays sexual pleasure as a part of spirituality, while other religions think of sex as evil.

Now, it seems the differences among religions are merely superficial, but also a matter of varying interpretations about human nature and life.

It's just so confusing.

But the cultured secular society also has sins. They also abhor drugs, sexual promiscuity, and selfishness. Civilized people tagged by Christians as secular are also normal people. They have successful careers, happy marriages, and faith in the future.

Happiness and bright hope for the future is not exclusive to Christians. Neither are the values and virtues of human life, and the sense of what's right and wrong. Or even spirituality.

Besides, when it comes to happiness, it looks like Christianity in particular, and religion in general, has a more pessimistic, mystical, and morose view of what happiness is.

Religion, instead of allowing people to discover what a happy life is personally, doggedly prescribes happiness in a less cheery way. And a happy life is not merely confined to religious people. In fact, most secular people appear happier than the religious.

When it comes to challenges in life, there's no difference between the religious and the secular. They are all equally subject to sickness, divorce, material lust, temptations of sex, accidents, and other tragedies in life.

So why should I be religious, or particularly Christian, when I could live and enjoy my life without the constraints of confusing beliefs? Besides, there is a dizzying number of them —all conflicting one another.

One prohibits attending the flag ceremony, for reasons of idolatry. Another forbids eating types of foods and insists on attending church on a particular day. Still another insists that speaking in tongues is the proof of conversion. Another one teaches that partaking of communion is a way to receive God's grace. Some believe in baptism by sprinkling, others by immersion.

But all require membership in good standing, as if their denominational registry were the exclusive registry into Heaven. Christian faith is nothing but a bunch of competing religious institutions, each wanting to dominate everyone—every one nothing but an exclusivist religious club.

So what's tagged as a holy Christian life is really nothing more than following a particular institutional policy based on

71

sectarian notions, biases, and prejudices intended to propagate denominationally-centered agenda.

Then why don't I just let go of my morose Christian outlook and just enjoy life as it is?

The hedonistic spirit crept even more into Frankie's soul. Then he made a drastic decision in life.

"I need to enjoy a life free from bothersome beliefs," he said enthusiastically. "I need to be free at last! What else can I do in life other than enjoy it?" He began looking forward to a new life of fresh adventures and new chapters in his search for meanings in life.

So he went out from his seclusion, peeped around his new world of fun, and bit by bit enjoyed the pleasures in the buzz of the night with mixed feelings of enthusiasm and anxiety, like a kid first learning how to ride a bike.

"Wow! This is just exciting," he exclaimed. "What a new, exciting life!" But after some intimate dances with gorgeous, alluring women and a few drinks, he began stumbling down.

"Take it easy, my friend," the man that greeted him earlier said. "I think you took it too hard the first time. Take it slowly. I guess you're new to this. Besides, this is not really your world," the man added.

Frankie fell down, and the man helped him back to his room. He stared at the man, looking like the Good Samaritan bringing a victim to the inn, only this time helping a man who'd fallen into pleasure back to his luxury suite.

The following day, Frankie awoke enthused again over the prospect of enjoying the rest of the week. Every night, he got better in enjoying his newfound life. The week passed by so quickly; how he wished he could have enjoyed more company of women, more booze, and more music, but the week frittered away.

Just before leaving to go back home, the seemingly suspicious yet sympathetic man offered his hand for a warm shake. "My friend, I hope you enjoyed your week. I hope you enjoy the rest of your life. Life, you know, is fleeting. So I hope you find what you're really looking for before it dissipates away."

Frankie hesitantly but warmly shook the man's hand, and the man then bid him goodbye.

After that, Frankie hunted for fun in life like never before. He casually dated one woman after another, usually meeting them in bars and at parties. And the more he sought enjoyment in life, the more he felt free from his previous sullen disposition.

One night, he reflected:

Perhaps the reason many Christians are becoming more secular is that they really never enjoyed Christian life. They, in their so-called faithfulness to God, were anxious about so many things. Anxious of hell, anxious of sins, anxious that the world might pollute their so-called moral purity. They're just so heaven-oriented that they forget to live life on Earth.

Or perhaps Christians just misconstrued the meaning of human life. By denying the pleasures in human life, they are actually denying the humanity of human life. Why should I deny myself pleasure when God has given me a body and senses so I can enjoy the pleasures of life? Hasn't God given me life so I can enjoy it socializing with my fellow human beings?

And look at what I had in the church: depression, an everyday fear of committing sin and keeping my delusional 'morality' pure, aside from sowing prejudice against others not belonging to my own denomination, hearing the bickering of church members, endless discussions about the so-called truths that were nothing but a perpetuation of one's opinion, and living in the fantasy of beliefs. Now, I enjoy life to the fullest.

~

Then, one day, he made another drastic decision. After dating several women, he impulsively proposed marriage to one. The lady accepted. Their wedding was set and planned. After getting lucky in a big-time real estate deal, he bought a luxurious house in an elite gated subdivision. He felt he was

74

at the top of the world. Young and financially stable, with a successful career, a gorgeous wife, and enjoying the fun and the luxury life offered.

~

But the time came that amid his restless insatiability for more pleasures and wealth, he began losing control of his life. The wife whom at the outset he married out of lust but later began truly loving, became pregnant and was filing for divorce, having found another man. He was deeply troubled and couldn't imagine life without her, more so without the child he truly longed to have.

His marital stresses caught him off-guard. The stress affected his job, his health, and his enthusiasm for life, until his career collapsed. He was seriously depressed and suffered from psychosomatic disease. He was also quickly losing what meager money he had left after his wife claimed more than half of it.

Then his dear mom suddenly passed away, and his beloved dad, too, was seriously ill.

Then his separated wife decided to abort their child. The bank also foreclosed on his house, and he ended up renting a cheap bachelor apartment far from the luxury he had enjoyed before. He became gravely ill as well, beset by chronic pain in his stomach.

Divorce is harsh, but when someone has a package of grave crisis situations in life—life is really broken. Frankie's life crushed bottom deep!

He reached out to his friends for help, but what he got was a mere superficial acknowledgment of his miseries. All left him alone and lonely. Having nowhere else to go and no one to cling to, he remembered God he had deserted years back.

He struggled over whether to pray or not, whether to believe in miracles or not, and whether God would still hear his prayers or not. After a while of struggling, he took the courage to pour out his miseries to the Heavenly Father he had once worshipped but had long since forgotten.

In loneliness, he pondered:

Is this what life on Earth is all about? A little time to enjoy it, then misery and death? I will just fade away, no more to be seen, no more to be heard, no more to keep company with my fellow human beings.

My friends and my wife have already left me. Now my mom is gone, and so is the child I dreamt to have.

My dad will be gone soon, and so will I.

I came to this world with nothing, and will depart with nothing.

The more he pondered, the more he realized the futility of life.

"Life is too short for me," he wept. "I'm only in my mid thirties and my life is about to end right here. Help me, please … I don't know what to do…I'm hopeless and helpless. And—uh! Nooo! I feel like taking my life now, so I won't have my misery anymore …"

But then, amid anxiety, dread, pain, and hopelessness, the picture of Jesus healing the sick, raising the dead, and finally dying just so he could assure humanity of new life, flashed in his mind.

"Jesus, if you healed the sick before, please heal me too. If you raised the dead before, please restore my life also. You know how I longed to find meaning in my life, but I went astray. I got lost. I'm full of heartache. My life is broken, I'm stricken by excruciating pain. The doctor believes I have colon cancer. I'm dying. My God and my savior, please save me. Please …" he begged Jesus as one groping in the dark, struggling to cling to one last hope of survival. Right after praying, excruciating pain struck him so severely that he writhed and screamed in pain. He called an ambulance and was rushed to the hospital.

~

The crucial time under the scalpel had passed. Minutes turned to hours, hours to days, and days to weeks. Those days his life was a blank slate. Those days, not only his body was recuperating, but also his soul.

~

"Hello, Frankie, remember me?" A man offered to shake Frankie's hand while he was lying on the bed. "Remember Sziget Festival?"

Frankie was trying to recall. "Oh, yeah! You're the one who took me back to the hotel that night when I got drunk."

"I'm actually a close friend of your dad, and also his lawyer. Remember, the rock singer who sang at your party after high school graduation, years back?" The man said.

"Hmm. Oh yah! The funny guy with a pony tail and a cool guitar that made us really laughed out loud. But you look more formal now with a short clean cut hair, as it was when I me you at Sziget." Frankie recalled.

"Well life change you know. And I'm going the extra mile for your dad because he went the extra mile for me also. He once saved my life. It's a long story, but anyway, he wanted to be sure that you're okay. After we met at Sziget, I've been trying to keep in touch with you. You've kept on moving like a gypsy. Your dad missed you for so long. He tried to contact you, but he couldn't find you, so it was up to me. Unfortunately, your dad passed away while you were in the ICU."

Tears trickled down Frankie's cheeks. He wished to have a heart-to-heart talk with his dad, but he'd procrastinated and now it was too late.

"Your dad loved you so much, Frankie, and I'm sure you also loved your dad. Your dad has acquired a number of properties, and also a significant savings that he intended to leave to you when he was gone. He had been saving for your future since your childhood days, even when you moved away from home to have your own life. I'm sure in about a week you'll be out of the hospital, so I came to see you and give you these keys and the papers. Your dad wanted to be sure that should you become broke, you still had a backup plan in life.

"Get well soon, my friend, and I hope you'll have a new life. I was also in tough times in life before, but your dad was a true friend who helped me go through it. Now it's my turn to help you. Should you need a helping hand, please let me know. Get well very soon." The man bade him goodbye.

Frankie reminisced on the wonderful moments he'd had with his dad and mom 'til he fell asleep—waiting for the day he could start anew.

~

He came back to the empty house where he'd grown up. He remembered the happy childhood days he'd had with his mom and dad and his friends. His beloved mom and dad were gone, so were his childhood friends. The town where he had grown up had changed. It had grown into a suburb.

After cleaning the house and getting nostalgic over the memorabilia, he groomed himself and strolled around the town, trying to remember the familiar landmarks of the town where he and his friends used to hang out.

It was his first day to explore the world again, the world he thought he'd never see anymore. The ambience of the world seemed fresh to him.

While strolling, he was amused watching a jovial young couple walking with two kids, one a boy and the other a girl. One was holding mom's hand, the other holding dad's hands while riding on his shoulders.

He smiled, imagining what his child would have been like if he had been born. He then wished to have his own happy family, too, someday.

He also saw a couple seniors sweetly walking together with love as fresh as their honeymoon. "Wow! That's the kind of love I wish I could have," he said wistfully. "True love, and sweet, as if it were at the beginning." He enjoyed watching the scenery of everyday life the rest of the day.

He beamed with tears of gratefulness. "I'm back to life again. Thank you, Jesus, for letting me realize how fragile yet precious life is. Now I entrust my life to you day by day, no matter what. Now I value the lasting matters in life more than the fleeting things." He talked to God like a child talking to his beloved, closest friend-father.

He also realized that prayer isn't just about asking for something from God; it's about conversing with Him like a son to a father and entrusting his life to Him so much so that every day he lived life with peace of mind.

"Now I have found the essence of Christian life. It's not merely about living up to the expectations of the church. It's about the daily experience of optimism and the peace of mind that comes from trusting God and living according to the values Jesus taught."

While saying that to himself, he felt that the deep-seated pressure in his soul was dissipating like steam, until it was finally gone. He felt engulfed by a fresh and verdant outlook on life.

Where marriage
is no longer hopeless

Marriage isn't just a social or sexual relationship...
It touches the very divinity of our ...

"Truly, as *The Washington Post* said, 'It's hard to remember you're still on planet Earth,'" Zoe said, captivated by the most exotic wonders of nature she'd ever seen. Majestic glaciers, portentous peaks, enchanting lava deserts, jovial geysers, rejuvenating geothermal springs, and enthralling scenery all mesmerized Zoe into an out-of-the-Earth paradise experience.

After cruising around Iceland, Zoe stayed in a hotel a stone's throw away from the vivifying Blue Lagoon. After dinner, she walked to the Blue Lagoon, and there, amid the enthralling full moon and steamy ambience, she found an oasis of calmness and healing of her soul and body.

"Nature, indeed, is the healer," she said to herself, engulfed by the ambience that soothed her weary soul and distressed body.

She thought the husband she'd trusted for years would always be there for her to heal her disenchanted soul, but instead he made her even more miserable and extremely anxious of what to do in life after having given up her career years back to take care of their family and support her husband, Benjie, in his ministry.

Now alone in the haven of nature, she found relief from the wretchedness of her failed marriage, the miasma of material lust, the humdrum of everyday life, the stresses of social hypocrisy, and the insanity of exploiting others for the advancement of her husband's whims and wishes. She felt that, deep inside, her soul was expelling emotional toxins and her body renewing itself into the kind of vivacious lady that she had been before.

"Ohhh!" she sighed, feeling the new life infused in her. She fell asleep soaking herself in a water of life with her head gently lying on a plank and her feet resting on another.

After an hour, nature had its own way of gently waking a nature-connected human that it had revivified, telling her it's time to go to bed, for tomorrow she'll have fresh vigor to face the grave challenges of life. Zoe woke up and walked back to the hotel, refreshed and beaming. That night, she fell asleep like she hadn't in years.

After a hearty breakfast of fresh foods, she went back to her room and sat on a wicker lounging chair overlooking a lagoon; then she began reminiscing on her happier days with Benjie, who was now becoming her ex-husband.

She remembered how she and Benjie had walked along the beach against the backdrop of the setting sun, sweetly holding hands, love binding them together. They looked like such a lovely couple dedicated to the sacred ministry of God, but as the years passed, the more their hidden natures had emerged.

"We were good at hiding our filthiness for years, but the more we reached the heights of fame and success, the more our secret life unraveled," she said, confessing the kind of life she wanted no more.

She could still recall the many times when throngs of people would applaud Benjie, as if out of the billions of people on Earth, he alone was the chosen oracle of God. She, too, was proud to stand by his side. The more people applauded them, the more material treasures poured into their cache. They were both jovial of the newfound wealth and fame they'd never expected.

She remembered Benjie used to joke, "Now we have a foretaste of Heaven ahead of other saints," pointing to the luxuries of life they were then enjoying.

Then the awakening came.

Zoe candidly confronted Benjie, feeling sorry and embarrassed that she, too, was part of a charade. "It's wrong. We've been deceiving people for years. We have exploited their consciences and commercialized faith. That's just disgusting!"

She took a sip of tea, then put the glass back on the side table and began reminiscing on the happier days when she and Benjie were together as man and wife. Those were the happy days that she missed, the days when they had lived a modest life.

Every Monday, they used to have family time with their preschool kids. She would imagine their fun picnicking and tobogganing, hiking, canoeing, or just window shopping in the mall or swimming in the indoor pool. It was a family full of fun.

Now she was struggling to find the answers for why their supposedly ideal family and marriage had been wrecked. She pondered on the enigma of marriage …

Why all the predicaments in marriage, despite its sacred blessings? Do church blessings really bestow sanctity and happiness in marriage? Or is it merely an outward show that really makes no difference in marriage, except for its superficial social glamour, which quickly dissipates?

If marriage is indeed divine, why the widespread outbreak of grievously displeasing divorces among Christians, even among their renowned ministers? Is the faith of those who claim to be the oracles of God on Earth merely a sham? Are they really channels of God's life-transforming power and blessings to humanity? If so, why can't that power transform their personal lives and bless their families? Or are they nothing but religious entrepreneurs who willfully exploit the consciences of their followers?

But what's really the very root of marital breakdown? Why can't couples transcend their petty conflicts? Why can't they be faithful, loving, and caring to each other and value the sanctity and happiness of their family? Why can't they be truly open to each other's souls, as they are to each other's bodies? It seems that openness to each other's bodies has become something perfunctory and cheap, while openness to each other's souls has become hush-hush, known only to a party outside the marriage bond.

And why the preoccupation with sex, as if sex is all there is in a man-woman relationship? Where's the place for care, altruism, and humanness in what's supposed to be the foundation of all human relationships? Is fulfillment in marriage still possible nowadays?

It seems faith in God is powerless to transcend the predicaments of marriage. Divorce is as common among Christians as it is among the secular, and so are extramarital affairs. No wonder many people today, both Christians and secular, opt for living together without marrying.

Has the 'til-death-do-us-part promise become a cheap, superficial cliché with no more profound meaning? Don't tell me that lifelong marriage commitment has already become a relic of the past?

Is there still hope?

My friends who are trying to stick it out seem happy, but I know they're hypocritical about what's really going on. Sooner or later, it will explode. It could have already if not for the embarrassment of maintaining the Christian tag branded on them. Or they're trying to endure the annoying pressures for the sake of their young kids. As soon as their kids are grown up, they'll be like birds rushing to be free from their cages.

But living together under one roof, pretending to love when there's actually no love, is just horrible. Has the world nowadays lost the sense of meaning of what marriage is all about?

But what really is the meaning of marriage anyway?

"Oh! What a conundrum!" She sighed and took another sip of her pure Viking tea, then continued reflecting on the marriage she had already lost, awaiting the legal confirmation to finally seal its brokenness.

"How did we end up like this?" she asked herself, hopeless after her tear-filled prayers for a couple years found no answer at all.

She reminisced on how it all began.

She and Benjie had met in a conservative Christian boarding school. She was brought up in the third generation of a conservative Christian family and dreamt of being a minister's wife. He was a newly converted Christian who changed his dream of becoming a rich medical doctor to becoming a humble pastor of God. She was a gorgeous young lady. He was a charming, gregarious young man.

They bumped into each other in a long line during enrollment. Somehow, the friction sparked a heat of first love that never seemed to die. They ate dinner together. Oftentimes, they would sit on a park bench overlooking the hills to watch the sun paint a romantic hue in the sky before it finally set. Before going home on vacation, they would get lost from the world to where they could be alone to savor the sweet nectar of love.

They fell in love, got married after graduation, and started a new family that they dreamed to carry over even to the hereafter. They were thrilled when Benjie finally got his ministerial call. They thought life then became not only fun, but also fulfilling.

Zoe smiled, remembering the thrills of exploring places around the world while serving God. She thought then that indeed God meant for them to be together the rest of their lives as a model couple who would lead many others to find the meanings of faith and family.

She remembered her mixed feelings of pain and excitement when their first baby was born. She watched him growing up in a happy family, though they did not have many material possessions then.

"Why can't that be again?" she asked herself, longing for those happy bygone days. "Why couldn't two people just enjoy life and be happy being together the rest of their lives? Why, God? Are You still there? Are you still working miracles in our lives today?"

Despaired, she let go of her troubled heart, wanting to be free like a pigeon ensnared in the cage of life's misery. She stood up, braced herself, smiled, and declared, "I still have a wonderful life ahead of me."

~

Meanwhile, Benjie was on the other side of the world, alone and deeply anxious about losing the material wealth and fame he enjoyed. It was the first time he'd had a holiday break alone. Looking back at his marriage, he began blaming Zoe.

"If only she wasn't a nagger, there could have been no squabbles. Ever since we got married, there were very few days where we didn't get to squabbling, and those were miraculous." He recalled those wrangling days ...

"Why can't you just listen to me?" he blurted.

"Why don't you listen to me?" she argued.

"You know what my greatest fear is? That the phenomenal success I have will crumble because of you. You, of all people, never truly supported me in my ministry."

"You know why you're afraid? You're afraid because people will know your secret," she retorted.

"What secret?" he screamed.

"You're a hypocrite! A deceiver! A liar! You want me to tell the world about you? You think I don't know you?" she responded, screaming also.

"Shut up! Do you think you would enjoy a life with this many blessings if not for me?"

The squabble was getting worse when the doorbell rang. At the door stood the head elder of the church they usually

90

attended when they were not out of town on their periodic crusades. They stopped squabbling and forced themselves to smile while greeting the visitor.

Oftentimes they were crabby, tense, and soulsick, and the more they were so, the more they reproached each other. Their marriage was a cycle of petty squabbling, calculated reproaching, and passionate self-vindication. As if petty matters really did matter. As if reproaching each other were cathartic. And as if self-vindication were self-fulfilling.

Ironically, after reaching the peak of their nonsensical conflicts, they would gravitate to the valley of endearment, sorry for what they'd done and pitying each other for the heartache they caused themselves. After saying sorry to one another, they would hug each other and reaffirm their "I love you's" and "I love you too's."

Then the romance and the sweet caresses would follow; he would appeal to her reason, and she to his emotion—for the happy marriage they both wished for.

In their sanity, both ardently wished for it. In their insanity, both zealously wished it crushed.

They didn't like the senseless phenomenon, but they couldn't understand why they kept on doing it until the senseless cycle reached the breaking point and their marital stresses became so tensed they exploded.

"Incompatible!" Benjie concluded. "We are just misfits! Our marriage is going nowhere."

"Yes! Because you just can't understand me. You ignore my feelings. You ignore me altogether, and I know why. Because you love that lady more than your wife and family," Zoe burst out, saying what she wanted to say for quite a time.

"I sacrificed my career to help you in your ministry and take care of our family, but you don't care at all. Your mind is blinded by lust. Not just lust of money and fame, but also lust of the flesh. This marriage is over! And I know you'll like it so you and your mistress can finally be together." Tears were trickling down her cheeks.

Their marriage broke down.

Zoe began doing what a lovely Christian lady never expected at the altar. She felt she still loved him, but she didn't want a miserable marriage the rest of her life. So she started working on their divorce.

Benjie also thought that having a new wife—sweeter, more inspiring, and more submissive than Zoe would make him happier and more fulfilled in life. He sought for a better woman and a better wife who he supposed would be the key to an even more prosperous life. By better, he meant characteristics in contrast with Zoe. He quipped, "Behind the greatest happiness of every man is the nicest woman."

He searched and explored, leaving his soon-to-be ex-wife in the house they had once enjoyed as a little Heaven on Earth.

Zoe struggled to find meaning in an empty house. She deeply longed for the presence of the loving husband she'd married years back. She recalled the laughter they'd shared, the prayers they'd said, and the life they'd once enjoyed, despite meager finances.

Now alone, she masqueraded, but deep in her heart she was still longing for him, just like when they'd first met. She realized, though, that the new Benjie had become more disgusting than any man she knew. Benjie was determined to let go of her and have a new family.

"Life is so empty. If only you knew how much I love you. Why can't you change back into the man I used to love?" she said.

But then, imagining Benjie sharing laughter and enjoying a life with his new wife, she resolved to face life with boldness and courage.

"I still have a life to live. I still have a son to take care of. If I give up, not only will I lose my life, but I will also lose my dear son. He's now the only human being I truly love, and I don't want to see him suffer like a homeless, abandoned child. I don't think Benjie even cares much for him. I need to take a break and heal myself," she resolved.

She decided to leave her son with her parents for a short break and take off for remote, enchanting Iceland.

~

After leaving the ministry, Benjie started a marketing business, then left the church to be free from prying eyes and lived with the lady he'd secretly had affairs with for some time. But after a year, they both realized they were not meant for each other, so he dated one woman after another, hoping that, by chance, he would find the ideal lady he was searching for.

After some time, amid the emptiness of life and anxiety of a dwindling business and draining finances, Benjie became seriously depressed and restless, bordering on a nervous breakdown.

With a depressed and restless soul, he remembered his pastor-friends from before and sought their help. Some encouraged him to move on with life. Others prayed with him. But he found them all merely courteous and no longer deeply concerned about him—an outcast no longer useful in the church.

"There's no place for a prodigal son in the church," he realized.

Both Benjie and Zoe were crying out for help, but their Christian friends, and the churches they'd once served were no longer interested in people who went astray like them.

Feeling lonely and helpless, and finding no spiritual recourse, Benjie decided to have a getaway far from the hassles and bustle of city life so he could meditate and think about his life and his future. He squeezed the meager money he had left out for what he foresaw could be something life-saving for him. He went alone to a "perfect refuge on Turtle Island."

Staring beyond the picturesque sunset, as if peering to see if the God whom he served before was still there amid the mess and restlessness of his life, he found himself soul-searching.

"I don't know what to do ..." he whispered in exasperation, as if subconsciously giving up and laying everything into God's hands.

While the island was filled with evening romance and happy families, his soul was filled with emptiness. He was trying to let go of his memories of Zoe, but in his soul those memories were still deeply etched.

Glancing at young romantic couples and happy families enjoying lovely evenings lit by enchanting moonlight in the backdrop of lush green hills and a tranquil white sand blue lagoon, where the gentle fresh breeze refreshed the weary, he remembered something.

"Yeah! We both forgot it! We're lost because we forgot it. I've got to find that box and bring it to her ..."

~

After his getaway, Benjie went to the cave in the mountain-top school where he and Zoe had first met and studied. After twenty-six years, the cave seemed different. He tried remembering where they had hidden the box. After about an hour of searching and clearing six possible spots, he was so thrilled to find it.

He dug out about a foot of topsoil and took out the stalagmite they'd used to cover the hole in the wall of the cave where they had hidden the box. The box was made of marble, and inside held their picture laminated in glass, taken on the day they'd fallen in love. On the back was the message with lines they'd alternately written. It said:

"We started it wrong—but we love each other, and the devil is waiting to break it. Someday when it comes—let's open this box and remember the promise we made. The promise—to truly repent, forgive each other, start a new life, and entrust everything to God's hands. No matter how dark it may get, God's light will always shine. Today we seal it with the thumbprint of our blood. We honor this as long as we live. Benjie & Zoe, June 9, 1988."

Benjie shed tears remembering the promise they'd made, realizing his mistakes. Right there in the cave, he cried to God and sincerely asked for forgiveness. He acknowledged and confessed all the sins he had committed, and with the most sincere prayer he had ever made, pleaded with God that if it be His will, to let him and Zoe start a new life again and enjoy the happy family they once had, even if it meant living on meager finances.

After the rendezvous with God in the cave, he felt the heavy burden he had carried dissipating from his heart. He felt so much lighter than before and began to see the world around him as bright and pleasant again. He beamed with newfound joy springing from deep within his soul, and then decided to go back home to Zoe.

~

Zoe came back vivified from her Blue Lagoon getaway. It was evening when she came home. After warming up the cooked seafood she'd brought from Iceland, she had dinner by candlelight, and afterwards took a warm bath in the Jacuzzi tub, went to bed, and fell asleep.

She dreamed of her bygone happy family days. The dream even took her back to her student days, when she and

97

Benjie had first met and become sweethearts. She saw the lovely romance they had, then she drifted back into a sound sleep.

Upon waking in the morning, the first thing she did was call her son, who was on a medical internship hundreds of miles away from home. It was Thanksgiving Day, and she missed him so dearly. Right after talking to him, the doorbell rang.

She opened the door, and it was Benjie, looking like a lamb while showing her the box. Immediately, it reminded her of the promise they'd once made. She was dumbfounded. Impulsively, she let Benjie come in.

They sat on the couch, and Benjie opened the box while Zoe was mesmerized. Benjie showed her their picture and read the promise on the back. Zoe's tears began trickling down her cheeks.

Sincerely, Benjie said, "I'm so sorry. I made a terrible mistake. I have sinned against God and you. I have already prayed to God. Now I'm here to ask for your forgiveness. I know I have done a terrible thing. I know I have hurt you so deeply. I have hurt our family. Please forgive me. I'd like to start a new life. And if you still wish, we can start a new life again." Benjie spoke in a soft voice that expressed the sincerity of his heart, with teary eyes beaming with love that pierced deep into Zoe's soul.

Zoe had to hug Benjie, and she shed tears over his shoulders. Benjie kissed Zoe on the cheek so sweetly and so true that it brought life again to the love they first had.

"I love you, Zoe," Benjie said.

"I still love you, Benjie," Zoe answered, with a bit of a choked voice.

Benjie wiped Zoe's tears, so did Zoe to Benjie, then the phone rang. Zoe picked it up. It was their son, Gideon.

"Oh, by the way, Mom, are you going to have turkey tonight? I know it's too big for you, but I found a restaurant there that delivers. I can order one for you."

"Sure, dear. And thank you for that," she replied. "And that's great, since I have someone here with me."

"What?" Gideon was puzzled. "Are you dating someone?"

"Well, he's here and would like to talk to you," Zoe said.

"Hello, Gideon!" Benjie said.

"Dad?!" Gideon was deeply surprised. "You're home with Mom?"

Zoe turned on the speaker phone.

"Yes, Gideon," Benjie replied. "Yes, Gideon, we're home. We're back home."

Gideon paused, with tears of joy. "I'm so happy, Dad, Mom. I've never been so happy as I am now. I'll order the turkey right away. I wish I could be there on Thanksgiving, but my heart goes out to you, Dad, Mom. I guess it's also good that you two can be alone this Thanksgiving night. I love you, Dad. I love you, Mom. And I would love to see us again as a happy family, just like when I was still a kid. Bye, Mom. Bye, Dad. I'll see you at Christmas, right in our own home."

"Sure, Gideon," Benjie answered.

"I cannot wait for that day, dear," Zoe replied.

Benjie and Zoe prayed together the most sincere prayer they've ever made. Thanksgiving night came, and the house that had been empty for years was again filled with true love and sweet romance.

~

Christmas came, and the family decided to sell their house in the new year and move to where Gideon would be working as a doctor. The New Year came, and in a month the house was sold. They moved to a new place, started a new life together, and began a new life's calling—a ministry to help couples discover or recover true love and a fulfilling family life.

One evening at a young couple's retreat at the elegant resort in Kananaskis, Benjie and Zoe testified. It was a retreat for young and successful professionals and entrepreneurs. Some were newly married. Others were contemplating. The rest were new sweethearts.

"We were once a young couple, like you. We loved each other, but we started it wrong, and we let that seed of a mistake grow in our marriage life until it destroyed what we used to cherish."

"I still remember what Benjie said when I asked him why he liked me when we first met. He said, 'because you're sexy,'" Zoe said.

"And I remember also when I asked her why she liked me, she said it was because I was charming," Benjie said.

"But what we actually meant was that we were sexually attracted to each other. It was all about sex, so we became sweethearts so we could have sex, then love each other later," Benjie pointed out.

"Instead of romance and expressions of care and noble love, what we had as soon as we became sweethearts was sex, despite the fact that we were then studying in a conservative Christian boarding school," Zoe added.

"We were shrewd enough to find ways to engage in our lustful desires. Mere sexual emotion, rather than the union of our souls, steered our relationship. Our relationship had only been on the level of the body rather than the soul, and we carried that over into our marriage life.

"And despite the fact that we had already learned to love each other, lust still haunted us and lingered throughout our marriage. Then, when I became a successful minister and proud of my fame and material blessings, the lust of the flesh haunted me again, this time with stronger propensity. I ended up shrewdly engaging and finding excitement in extramarital affairs," Benjie testified.

"Then our marriage and family life began crumbling down. The little wrong things we did day by day piled up into a huge mess. We cuddled lust instead of nurturing love. Vehemently argued instead of lovingly communicating. Eagerly justified each other's mistakes instead of kindly listening and patiently forgiving. Zealously hated each other for the mistakes done instead of guiding ourselves to the right path. Blamed each other's differences instead of understanding each other's individuality," Zoe said.

"We masqueraded ourselves with our superficial Christian personae, but deep within our marriage was a devilish, sinful bondage. We hid our sins behind the facade of superficial holiness and deceived the people around us," Benjie confessed.

"But God was gracious enough to change our lives in an unexpected way amid our brokenness. We thought our marriage was hopeless, but in our loneliest moments, God guided us back to each other to discover what true love is and recover the promise we made years back. We never thought the promise would be prophetic and providential. God was so gracious that even early in our relationship, He provided us with something to return to in case we drifted away in the future," Zoe testified.

"Marriage isn't just a social or sexual relationship, neither merely a religious ritual. Marriage touches the very divinity in our humanity—the image of God. The image of God as the Trinity is the image of profound relationship. Perfectly one, harmonious, and fulfilled within each inner circle. From that relationship springs the true joy of having a family."

"Our marriage is not yet perfect, but it's now directed by nobler values in life that make marriage and family life very fulfilling. We've discovered the essence of marriage—the deepest human relationship bonded together by noble love, mutual care and kindness, deep friendship, and commitment to create a happy family," Benjie expounded.

"And don't forget to make the promise to truly repent, forgive each other, start a new life, and entrust everything in God's hands," Zoe said, beaming with a bright outlook on life. "Engrave it and seal it with something memorable, then put it inside the box that will last a lifetime so that when the time comes, one of you can open it to remind each other of the sealed promise you once made. Remember, no matter how dark it may get, God's light will always shine."

Where prayer
is no longer faithless

*Payer is not just about asking God something.
It's the spontaneous ...*

*I*ntrigued by the spirituality of the East, Max decided to see and feel Tibet. Upon arriving, he was immediately amazed by the topography, the nature, and the people of Tibet.

Wandering around the Potala Palace, he was awed by the thousands of shrines and statues that majestically soared toward the vastness of Heaven, but his spirit was somewhat mesmerized by the most sacred place in Tibet: Jokhang Temple, the seat of Tibet's spirituality. The mystical reverberations of the prayer bells amid the whistling wind and the serenity at the top of the world enthralled him.

"What a strange place to seek God and pray for his will," he said to himself.

Seeing a meditating monk, he looked for a spot where he could be alone to gaze upon the sky beyond the majestic mountains and silently talk to God, who seemed not to answer him anymore. He'd begun delving into the faith he had once fervently believed in, but now doubted.

He pondered ...

Does prayer still work today? I've been begging God to answer my needs for years since, but He hasn't. In fact, my life is getting worse than before. I'm not asking Him for luxuries. All I'm pleading for is the healing of my life, for Him to bring me back to the calling I believed He had for me, to which I dedicated my life. And also to restore my broken family.

But did prayers really work in my life before? Or were what I presumed God's answers to my prayers simply coincidences, if not the natural results of what I did? If He answered my prayers before, why not now, when I need it most? I have already repented of my conscious and my unwillful deeds.

Besides, I believe my conscience is clear. It was my wife's habitual propensity for extramarital relationships that caused all these miseries in my life and the breakdown of our happy family. Now that she's finally moved in with that already married man, the more she's been blessed, while the more I suffer.

Her polygamous husband, too, seems to enjoy a prosperous life while I'm alone and lonely with a broken career, rejected anywhere I go to find a livelihood—and becoming poor. How long can I endure such unfair hardships in life?

Yes, the Bible says that God answered the prayers of His people in the past. He even showed them astounding and life-changing miracles. But what about in the present? And what about for me? Is God far from humans now? Or is He just far from me? Or were the so-called answered prayers and miracles simply myths, either mythical stories or symbols of the ancients' personal and societal wishes?

Probably prayer is simply a psychological tool for believers to develop a sense of hope and confidence as they face the challenges of life. Or in another sense, a form of catharsis to let off steam regarding the pressures of life. Although it could result in peace of mind because of the temporary break from stress, it doesn't really result in miraculous divine interventions. Of course, in that restful break, one may have a clearer mind on how to cope in life without necessarily implying God's miracles.

If God's miracles were real in the Bible times, why are they not happening today? Is it because of faith? But what's faith? And what's the difference between the faith of the people in the olden days and the faith of people now? When people pray to God nowadays, they pray to him because they believe in him. Otherwise, they won't pray at all.

But what is faith anyway: an intense form of positive thinking? A deep sense of illusion that what one wishes will be realized? Or just a passive acceptance of fate? Does all the screaming and emotional outpouring in church really work? Or is it nothing but a means of temporary emotional relief from worshipers' emotional pressures that don't really effectively invoke God miracles more than classic, silent prayers?

Yes, some people claim they were healed during worship filled with emotional trances caused by wild music, screaming prayers, moving testimonies, and belief in the power of a self-claimed healer. But c'mon, if these are real, believers in particular—and humanity in general—wouldn't need hospitals anymore. Yes, there could be the healing of psychosomatic diseases, but in the same way that the body gets sick when the mind is stressed, the body also heals when the mind is freed from stress and filled with a bright outlook on life. It's nothing miraculous. It's just the law of nature.

And why are there no more angels today, confirming God's will for His believers? There must be an answer to all of these enigmatic questions. Probably, like most believers, I have the wrong concept of what prayer really is. I usually think of prayer as asking God for something I wish for, but what if prayer is not really about asking God, but something else?

108

Yeah ... amid this material world, I think of God as a genie who could grant my wishes—a genie-god. And what if prayer is indeed miraculous, but what I usually mean by prayer is not what God meant? If so, what's it all about? And how should I really pray?

Max went to Tibet to explore its mysteries, but the mystical ambience of Tibet somehow drew him to profoundly ponder on his faith. And, being drawn deeper into the mystery of faith, he found more questions than answers, more questions that could leave him faithless if not answered.

"Max? Is that you?" a senior who looked even more robust than the middle-aged Max asked in surprise.

"John? My old time friend and mentor. Good to see you here," Max responded.

"I thought I saw you walking towards the palace when I came out from the minibus. Now I know it's really you. C'mon, let's see some more things around." John gently tapped Max's shoulder, cheering him up, sensing Max's anxious actuations.

The two friends further explored the hidden mystical treasures that are Tibet.

~

After the trip to Tibet, Max's quest for the meaning of prayer still lingered in his mind and haunted him.

Max had experienced what he had regarded as God's answer to his prayers, but in the years since his wife had left him and he, too, had left the pastoral ministry, he'd begun to lose faith in prayer. He'd tried reading and listening to Christian books, watching inspirational films, and attending varied churches, but he found them all vain. He'd even amusingly tried different methods of praying propagated by modern day self-proclaimed prophets of God, but found them silly.

He compelled his mind to think and believe that prayers still worked, but he found himself not just losing faith in prayers, but also losing faith in God. He was anxious over what would happen to him and his two kids with his long years of joblessness, a sick body, and having no family to lean on. He depended on the meager tax benefit and fees he received from renting the vacant rooms of his house. He was anxious he wouldn't be able to sustain paying the mortgage anymore. He shivered, imagining being a homeless single dad with two young kids.

He prepared well for his career and got a number of educational credentials, but no church, para-church, or Christian school was true-hearted enough to use his talents,

110

given that he was a divorcee, and a stranger from another church, even if a true-hearted Christian. More so, as usual, he belonged to a cultural minority whose capabilities were always demeaned by the dominant Caucasian Christian leaders and believers.

He thought that if Christianity were indeed the faith of Christ, it should be life-changing enough to take away ethnic prejudice, bias, and segregation. He also realized that while the secular world was getting more inclusive, Christianity still remained very exclusivist and discriminatory.

"Where's the answer to the prayer of Jesus himself that his people may be one?" he asked, deeply troubled.

Not finding the answers to the deepest longings of his soul, he let go of his faith. Not just faith in the power of prayer, but also faith in the credibility of Christianity. He looked closely at non-praying, non-churchgoing secular people and saw in them happy marriages and family lives, successful careers, and stable finances. And they were also healthy.

He reflected ...

I thought only Christian believers were supposed to have prosperous, happy lives. Happiness and fulfillment in life are not reserved for Christians—it's a common gift of God to every-one.

But is it really a gift from God, or simply fate that others are destined to enjoy life while others not? There are billions of hard working people in this world, but why only a few billion-aires? Is life in this world really directed by God? Or is every-thing just a matter of fate or luck?

But if it's fate, nobody knows about it until he or she is there ...

No! I don't believe in fate; that doesn't make sense. Luck, probably. Indeed, some are luckier than others. Perhaps in-stead of praying, I should just believe that luck will come to me one of these days and I should keep trying. It seems there's really no difference between belief in luck and belief in prayers.

But whatever it should be, I've got to move on. I have kids to take care of. They've pinned their hopes on me. I should be-lieve in myself and make my kids proud that despite serious challenges in life, I can still successfully raise them up. From this time on, I will be courageous and think of life in a more positive way.

Finding prayer no longer relevant in his life, he ceased praying, but not totally. He ceased it as a routine, but at times he would say a sentence or two in bed just to let off the steam of his anxiety. After prayer, he would assert his courage in facing life.

"No more fear," he declared.

With prayerlessness came faithlessness. A life without prayer ended up in a life without faith. Christianity became to him just another system of beliefs, no different than a philosophical or political belief. It was in some sense functional and useful, but not a necessity in his personal life anymore.

"The seculars could have been right in saying that humans are the captains of their own lives," he thought.

He took charge of his own life without regularly resorting to divine help, and life seemed okay for some time. He also seemed to get physically better. He got temporary jobs here and there that at least augmented his meager income."

He beamed with self-confidence. "See, life is a just a matter of taking it easy and doing the little things that need to be done every day. Someday, I'll find myself back to full life again, even fuller than I was before."

~

But one night, unexpectedly, an intense dream overwhelmed him. The dream was so real that he struggled to believe it was just a dream while he was in it; it felt real. He felt the deep agony of losing his kids. He looked for them everywhere, but they were nowhere to be found, and wherever he asked for help, nobody seemed to care.

"They're the only humans I loved. They're the only inspiration I have in life. Please help me find them." He begged for help from everyone he met, but everyone ignored him. He couldn't bear the heartache of losing his kids. He wailed in despair: "I can no longer see them." The fun and the sweet memories he'd had with his kids flashed back, as if he were in the second dimension of a dream state.

"Please!" he screamed. "Does anybody see my kids? Please, help me!" he begged again, this time so much more desperate than before.

He was frightened and lonely. Then, in extreme fear, the dread of death also lurked over him. He felt that his body was weak; he was severely shivering and saw himself emaciated and dying.

Then he saw his kids taken away by a family that looked rude and mean, with the dad beating his kids. The kids were screaming in pain while pitifully trying to reach out their hands to Max. They cried, "Daddy, please help!" Max tried to stand up and help, but he was too weak to even move his body.

Feeling helpless and hopeless, he fell frustrated to the ground, weeping. He tried to scream for help but found himself unable to utter a word. All he could do was weep while staring at his kids again. He wept because he deeply loved and cared for them and was losing them. The scene was too much for him to bear, and he fainted.

Silence and emptiness lurked for a few moments, then, while still sobbing like a helpless and hopeless child, he saw Jesus asking him if he truly loved his children. With deep sincerity and a sobbing voice, he answered yes, then plead-ed, "Please give them back to me."

"That's what I feel when somebody takes you away from me. Remember what you said when you first dedicated your life to me?" Jesus asked.

Max shook his head.

"You said, 'When life gets tough, just give me the faith tried in the fire,'" Jesus said.

Max remembered. He nodded, affirming with eyes blurred by tears.

"I know deep in your heart, though you seemed to wan-der away, you still have that faith in me, and you're strug-gling to make sense out of it all. Now I come to intervene so I won't lose you. I offered my life for you because I love you, my dear son. In the same way that you have sacrificed yourself to take care of your kids because you deeply love them, I love you, too, and don't want to see you lost from me."

Max woke up sobbing, then looked to both sides of the bed and realized it had only been a dream. He kissed his sons, then knelt on the bed and lay hands on them, praying to God like he never had before. He prayed that they would always be together, safe and happy. He asked God for forgiveness, talked to him like a son talking to a father, and entrusted his and his sons' lives to God.

He realized what prayer meant. It wasn't just about asking something of God. It's the spontaneous, enjoyable, and fulfilling private moments with God that spring forth from an intimate creature-Creator relationship, just like the spontaneous, enjoyable, private moments between a caring father and his son, a loving couple, or the best of friends.

He felt one with God that night like never before. One in heart, and one in spirit. He was reconnected with the root of his being and existence. Max had never felt a full release of burden before that night. He'd never slept so soundly before that night, and he awaited bright new days ahead.

Where God's will no longer fails

*God's will is not about attributing to God
what happens in our lives, either tragic or blissful.
It's about the divine gift of ...*

The serene, yet astonishing wonders of nature around Yellowstone National Park were the perfect setting for Joy to find the healing she longed for.

Watching the spectacular eruption of the Old Faithful Geyser, the breathtaking scenery of Lower Falls and Yellowstone Grand Canyon, and the magnificent Mammoth Hot Springs, reminded her that there were still hidden treasures of life beyond the humdrum of everyday life engrossed in material insatiability. It was a well-spent day for her, and the evening was just so lovely and restful.

After breakfast, Joy sat on the lounge chair overlooking a tranquil lake. There, in the ambience of the quiet blue lake and the vastness of the clear sky adorned by gently moving white clouds that seemed to portray a shepherd gently carrying a lamb in his arms, Joy wondered if she'd find the healing she'd been longing for.

She watched the shepherd in the sky until it was gone, then she looked back on her life's journey and reflected on what God's will really meant. Questions that seemed trivial to her before now took on serious considerations ...

Is it really God's will for Christians to live prosperous lives? I mean prosperous in the sense of the wholeness of life, not just materially and physically, but also emotionally and spiritually.

Yes, as a successful entrepreneur, I am financially blessed and enjoy the luxuries of life more than an average person. I'm also physically healthy with a good sense of humor and a seemingly happy outward disposition in life.

People around me think I'm indeed the happiest person in the world. They don't know that deep within me is a depressed, materially insatiable, restless soul who always feels insecure as to whether God will continually bless me more. They don't know that not only am I suffering from depression, but also addicted to anti-depressant drugs that I cannot live without.

118

And now, my depression and addiction is about to implode my life into pieces.

My mom passed away without us having a heart-to-heart talk. Now my dad is also sick and dying and has lost faith in God's miracles. He still refuses to talk to me when I visit him. Why can't he just forgive me?

Yes, it was my fault I procrastinated when he asked me to come and visit Mom before she passed away. Yes, I lingered, if not ignored him outright, not wanting to miss what I thought would be the biggest business deal I ever had.

Dad thought I really didn't care for them at all, that all I cared about was money. And he might die, too, without us having that precious moment together.

Thinking about death reminded Joy of the death of her husband a few years ago. It was his death that she thought she had already learned to accept, believing it was God's will. But that death still haunted her every now and then. She missed him so dearly. She tried believing that God always has a divine purpose for everything that happens in a believer's life, but losing him made her doubt if that was indeed so.

"What if, indeed, everything just happens without God behind it all?" she asked, questioning her faith.

She couldn't accept the fact that it was God's will that the man she loved so dearly and depended upon for guidance in life would be taken away from her.

She pondered ...

Why is there sickness and tragedy among Christians, as it is among non-believers? Yes, God promised the new Heaven and the new Earth, but what about life in the present? If present life is part of the future eternal life, why can't believers at least have a prescient foretaste of that life in the hereafter? Why reserve everything in the today when life now could be as real as life in the future?

I don't see the wisdom in having a miserable life in the present and holding back happiness for the future. This doesn't make sense. And how sure are believers that indeed they will inherit that blissful life forever, and not others? Or as some pastors have said, 'only God knows and only God judges,' so how sure am I and the rest of Christians that only we will be saved? What about if it turns out that the so-called non-believers will also be saved? And worse, if the so-called Christians will be lost to God's kingdom instead?

And why does humanity, including those who believe God has already saved them, need to suffer? Are sin and the Devil powerful enough to override God's gracious will for a blissful life on Earth? Has the Devil taken over God's sovereignty over human life and the universe? It just can't be. For God is God and ever will be God. God is the one in control.

But why the miseries in life? Is it because of human choice? Of course, all humans would normally choose happiness, health, and prosperity. No one ever likes misery, neither sin nor the devil.

Is there such a circumstance so overwhelming that even God can't cope with it? I don't think so. God is all-powerful. But why hasn't he fixed the problems in human life? What constrains him from doing so?

Joy was troubled.

She'd grown up in a Christian country and a Christian home that believed that God takes care of human beings, especially His people. Though she came across the issues of holocaust, genocide, famine, the horrors of war, natural catastrophe, sickness, accident, and death, she didn't take these undesirable and uncontrollable phenomena into deeper consideration before now.

"Where was God in all these? What happened to the fulfillment of His will on Earth as it is in Heaven?" she asked, deeply troubled.

She'd studied the Bible and had thought she knew it all. For years, she'd preached and taught God's will for His people. In times of misery, she was ever-ready to comfort the bereaved. She assured them that God still had a plan in their lives and that He was still in control. But the toll of doubts took her to the point where she could no longer bear seeing tragedies one after another, as if really there was no God who managed life on Earth.

One event after another kept piling up in her soul. Her best of friends was diagnosed with stage IV breast cancer. The couple she depended on so much for her business after her husband passed away unexpectedly filed for divorce on the grounds of the wife's extramarital relationship. Joy's young professional son and daughter no longer believed in God. She was also under investigation for tax evasion. A lawsuit had also been filed against her because of the death of a senior woman in the spa resort she owned. Her other friends, too, were staying away from her.

She was so anxious that her once-booming spa resorts would one day crumble down and she would lose not only her prestige, but also her wealth. She couldn't bear imagining the time when people would talk about her as a once-wealthy businesswoman with celebrity status now bankrupt and poor.

The boyfriend she had been dating for about a year, and had fallen in love with suddenly, had decided to take a job in a foreign land far away from her. Loneliness, confusion, doubts, and fear of the future engulfed her.

She foresaw the looming death of her dad, who still refused to talk to her. Her dad had suffered two strokes before, but he was able to recover. Ever since then, he had gotten weaker and weaker. She had a foreboding that this time he wouldn't survive and would carry with him to his death his deep, unresolved ill will against her. She, too, was fearful that sooner or later she might die of a drug overdose if she didn't overcome her nasty habit, which had burgeoned after her boyfriend had left.

Troubled and tired, she fell asleep on the lounge chair. Upon waking up in the morning, the first things she saw were lofty pine trees. Then she realized the message nature was telling her—evergreen in the summer, as it is in the winter; ever alive in the spring, as it is in the fall.

"Thank you, God, for giving me hope," she beamed. "Now show me the miracles."

She went back home after her Yellowstone getaway with glowing hope that something good was going to happen to her.

Upon arriving home, she checked her mailbox and found a letter. It was from her boyfriend. Thrilled, she opened it, and it was a lovely Valentine's card.

"Yes!" she exclaimed, gesturing with both arms, and kissing the card.

Upon entering the house, she noticed the answering machine blinking. She played the message and it was her dad calling her to come so they could talk. "Yeah!" she exclaimed again with hands raised, praising God for the miracle.

Then the phone rang; it was her son, telling her that he and his sister had decided to try church again. After talking to her son, the phone rang again, as if the mail and all the phone calls had been orchestrated by divine providence. The next call was from her lawyer, telling her that the family of the senior who was suing her spa had decided to drop the case to find peaceful rest for their mom. They realized their mom had at least died in the comfort and restfulness she'd been seeking. More good news after the other followed.

"I can't believe it! What an outpouring of miracles!" she exclaimed, raising up her hands

Amid the showers of blessings, her soul began healing, until she found no more propensity for drugs and was enveloped with a cheerful outlook on life again.

Then she realized what God's will meant. It wasn't about attributing to God what happens in our lives, either tragic or blissful. Nor was it about attributing to God what we intend to do, as if God approves it. It was about the divine gift of the will to live—the courageous spirit amid the odds of life, the creative willpower to rebuild life when broken, and the bright constructive disposition in everyday life.

"It's God's will for Christians to live life on Earth just like any other human being, but with a different outlook on life. An outlook of being evergreen—hopeful beyond odds, enthused of life despite the challenges, courageous while others give up, and able to take a break from the stresses of life and bounce back again with fresh energy. Evergreen in the summer, as it is in the winter of life. Alive in the spring, as it is in the fall."

Where divine calling is no longer delusional

Divine calling is not merely about choosing a career.
It's about making a ...

T'was a life-changing mountaintop experience for Ricki.

Atop the soaring Christ the Redeemer statue on Corcovado Mountain, overlooking the delightful city built around one of the most sought-out beaches in the world, dotted by gorgeous mountains, Ricki's spirit hovered while his soul wandered like a lost traveler. Gazing at the vast blue sky above, he remembered how once he had been sure God was guiding his life. Then, staring at the city below, he reminisced on the people he had ardently aspired to lead to God.

He once dreamt of serving God the rest of his life. Now, though still finding some meaning in faith, he had already lost his sacred vocation, and though he already had a high-paying job, his soul was still restless, seeking a calling that could be fulfilling, but he didn't know what.

He pondered ...

Is there really such a thing as a divine calling? Does God still have a purpose for my life? If there is, how can I know it? If there's none, why doesn't He let me know? Or is life just a matter of the choices I make every day?

Yes, people make mistakes in life, but no one really wishes to make mistakes. Normal people just want to live a good life. No one really wants to be bad.

It's the uncontrollable circumstances in life that make people bad or good. It seems that everything in life indeed happens by chance. Even the decisions I make seem to randomly emerge without divine intention. Life is so confusing.

And now I'm beginning to doubt if God is really guiding everyone's lives, including mine. Why, for example, do many innocent people die as victims of crime, accidents, and natural disasters, while many greedy exploiters and corrupt people enjoy prosperous and safe lives?

Was it God's purpose that my friend, a dedicated and well loved small city pastor, his wife, and young kids, died in a tragic accident caused by a reckless drunk driver while greedy Wall Street CEOs that caused hundreds of thousands of people to lose their jobs and homes enjoy luxurious, healthy, happy, and safe lives?

Is it God's purpose that millions of innocent children and mothers will brutally die at the hands of a tyrant dictator while the tyrant enjoys fulfilling his lust for wealth, women, wine, and power?

It's ridiculous to believe, as my church pastor said when I was first converted, that God is behind the rise and fall of the rulers of the world. So God, in his love and all-encompassing powers, planned the rise of tyrants that dehumanized societies? This doesn't make sense at all.

Or has God simply created humans with capabilities both to build and destroy life, then left them to choose which course of action to take?

"Oh! God, I'm confused about life." Ricki sighed like a man falling into the abyss of gloom, struggling to cling on with his last strength left to what he thought was his last anchor in life.

Confused, he reminisced on his life's journey and how he ended up in a life of confusion ...

A couple months after baptism, he made a radical decision in life, believing it to be God's will. Not only did he decide to be religious, he also changed careers. He left his childhood dream behind. His dad wanted him to be a medical doctor, and he, too, was enthused about it, both for the prestige and the good money careers in medicine offered.

He'd wanted that his whole life, but conversion to a particular church drastically changed his interests. He thought saving people's souls was more important and nobler than healing one's body, so he decided to be a pastor. And not just an ordinary pastor, but a pastor-theologian. He left halfway through his medical studies and shifted to theology.

After finishing graduate studies, he was called to a pastoral ministry. His ministry, both to the church and the community, was fruitful. He conducted successful evangelistic crusades and led citywide multi-sectoral programs, one of which caught headlines in a national paper. People were baptized, the church grew, and he even planted a couple more churches.

But then his inclusive Christian attitude caught the ire of his church's bureaucracy, which believed that close relationships, more so of joint evangelistic community endeavors with other denominations, was a grave heresy. His insistence that there was nothing wrong regarding varied denominations as all belonging to one universal family of Christ on Earth, as well as that working together could enhance Christian faith and ministry in a secular world, resulted in a serious bureaucratic conflict that threatened his cherished pastoral ministry.

The fundamentalist president warned him of the consequences should he not change his inclusive attitude. But Ricki ignored the warning. Upset, the president began spreading ill will against Ricki among his bureaucratic colleagues. The bureaucratic pressure on Ricki became unbearable, and he was about to implode.

Then, the conference president put Ricki's ordination on hold and even threatened to discipline him if he didn't change his trans-denominational attitude. His passion for the universal communion of separated churches seemed undying. He believed that the church is the universal people of God regardless of superficial denominational affiliations— so churches need to transcend their self-centered enclave and join together to fulfill the common mission of guiding people to find meanings in their lives.

Then, Ricki was summoned to his denomination's head office for a disciplinary meeting on the grounds that he had not repented from working with heretics and bringing heresy into the church. So, to avoid the disciplinary measures, Ricki was ordered to desist his heretical attitude; otherwise, he would be disciplined for a period of time until he finally repented of his sins, or worse: he would be forced to resign from the pastoral ministry.

"On what grounds are you imposing discipline on me?" he flared up. "I committed neither sexual immorality nor negligence in my responsibility. In fact, the church is growing. The community has learned to love our local church more. Our church is becoming more significant to the life of our community."

"Insubordination and heresy!" the president bellowed.

Then Ricki made a defense of his faith that echoed Martin Luther's testimony in the Diet of Worms.

Insubordination, because I wanted our church to be more like the original universal church? Heresy, because I'm more concerned with the personal salvation of people and the spiritual well-being of the community rather than propagating our sectarian eccentricities?

Pastoral ministry is not primarily about propagating our denominational institutional expansion. It's about leading people to Christ so they can experience salvation and live a new life. It's about serving the community. It's not about exploiting people to serve our selfish denominational agenda.

Haven't you seen that except for a few fundamentalist members in my church, most church members are happily and actively supporting me? Are you that insecure that you fear cooperating with other denominations will make prospective converts join other churches? Oh c'mon, if we truly believe that

131

our denomination offers the truth and something more meaningful to the life of the community, people will naturally join our particular spiritual family.

This is no longer the Medieval Ages, when the church did little more than exploit people's consciences so the church could further increase its material and political gains. We now live in an educated postmodern world where people choose what's meaningful for them.

Our task is to make the gospel relevant to the everyday lives of people in this challenging time. Every day, people are confronted with varied challenges in life. The last thing they need is a church that tells them it has the only secret of Heaven.

Or are you just frightened by the thought that people will realize that we don't hold exclusive rights to Heaven and hell? C'mon, guys, if you truly have a sincere conscience, open up your mind to the fact that Christ is universal, and his church, his people, are trans-denominational.

You should all realize that sectarianism was not Christ's, but the result of numerous cycles of self-centered, oftentimes brutal, preoccupations of church leaders to control others. Christ did not establish the many denominations that we now have. People who either had materialistic or egocentric interests did.

132

"Enough of your heresy! You have become even worse than we suspected. That's the result when you associate with heretics. You, yourself, become a heretic also," the president bellowed again.

Ricki responded.

A heretic?

You call someone who wishes to come back to the original nature of church ministry and Christian faith as in the days of the early apostles a heretic?

That's ridiculous!

Wake up! Open up your minds. Think outside the box. See that truth is much larger than our sectarian notions. Haven't you seen the irony that while we profess the universality of Christ and his church, we still persist in our exclusive disposition?

We don't hold the exclusive rights to God and Heaven. God is much larger than us. Heaven is not reserved for a particular religious organization. It's reserved for the new humanity—the whole transformed human race.

"Are you saying that other churches are also true? And they could also be the way to Heaven?" the ministerial director asked.

"Of course!" Ricki replied.

"Ricki, you're really getting deeper into apostasy. If you will not recant what you said and truly repent of your apostasy, we don't need to discipline you anymore. We need to expel you from this church.

"You're polluting the purity of this church. You're demeaning its sanctity. There is no other church on Earth that Christ approved other than this church. This is the only remaining true church on Earth, and this church is the only way to Heaven.

"Now," the chairman of the board said, "I ask you to recant and repent, or we shall immediately expel you without further warning. I have dedicated my entire life to preserving the purity of this church, and I don't want to see anybody, more so a young budding minister like you, threaten its integrity,"

Ricki responded:

Dedicating your entire life?

So am I! I left my promising medical career to sacrifice myself in the ministry of God, to serve people and help them find meaning in their lives. Don't tell me what dedicating a life to God is.

If only all of you could realize that you're trapped in your entrenched, illusory notions, then you would see that indeed there is sense in what I'm passionately trying to tell you.

It's not about us. It's about the people we serve and the universal God we worship.

He said this in desperation, but he continued expounding on his faith with zeal and purity of heart.

The beliefs we have did not come fresh from God. They were carried over from previous traditions. And what we regarded as our unique truths are simply the products of human reflection, which, after finding consensus among our organizational pioneers, were regarded as the truth.

Each denomination does that. So Christianity is filled with all sorts of conflicting notions about God and the way to salvation. Why? Because Christians ended up obsessed with propagating the varied and divisive eccentric notions they created. Instead of coming together as one family of Christ to fulfill the common mission he entrusted to us, we've obsessed over controlling Heaven and making it our exclusive domain. In our selfishness and arrogance, we would rather see other Christians go to hell than see us all together journeying to Heaven.

"This is the second time I said enough!" the president exclaimed. "Now, we ask you to sneak out while we deliberate on your termination."

135

"Termination?" Ricki replied. "No need. Consider me now resigned from my pastoral ministry from this time onward! And I'd like you to take my name out of the church membership. I don't believe in this church anymore."

His staunch stance on what he believed as true, tempered by his impulsiveness, led him to the edge of a crushed career he'd once thought of as a noble dream.

He resigned from the ministry he'd once dreamt of as his lifetime vocation. He left the church he'd once imagined he'd serve the rest of his life deeply disheartened by its dogged exclusivism. His decision was abrupt and surprised the local open-minded church members who enthusiastically supported him.

Having nowhere else to go, having no other qualifications except theology, he applied for a teaching post in other Christian universities and seminaries he thought were open-minded and inclusive. For years, he doggedly sought his new teaching dream, only to be rejected year after year, despite numerous openings that rightly fit his qualifications.

Then he realized that what he thought were open-minded and inclusive Christian universities and seminaries were nothing but masquerades. He discovered that beyond the masquerade of even the so-called liberal Christian learning institutions was a deep-seated sectarian mentality compounded by ethnocentrism.

He realized that the theological academe was elitist, with cultural minorities relegated to the fringes. The so-called theologians were nothing but absolutist ivory-tower philosophers no different than the absolutist denominational bureaucrats he'd encountered in his past pastoral ministry. The only difference he saw was in the way they spoke about God and Heaven.

His pastoral dream was shattered, and now his teaching dream was also crumbling down, until he lost hope of coming back to Christian service. He regretted insisting on his conviction of being an inclusive Christian, which had led him to lose a stable livelihood. Now he was a wanderer, with no church he could call home, no spiritual family to support him, jobless, and with little money left in his savings account.

Desperate, and feeling deeply betrayed by religion, at times he thought of taking his own life, but the thought of seeing his beloved dad and mom grieving for his tragic death restrained him. Having no choice but to move on in life, he struggled to find whatever job he could. But having no skills or experience except pastoral work theology, he was always bypassed by others, even by foreigners hired for their lower wages and connections with an international network of exploitive placement agencies. He lived on welfare for years.

137

He moved on in life, spending a portion of his meager remaining money to get training in human resources. Then one day, the news about the opening of a new and innovative corporation with a fresh people-centered culture and keenness for developing employees was heralded in town. He was enthused. He applied and highlighted his transferable skills. He was called for an interview, and his wish for a decent livelihood was granted. He was hired.

There, he poured out afresh the enthusiasm he'd once had for the ministry. After saving money, he pursued further professional education on top of the corporate professional training he had undergone. The corporation noticed his productivity and potent for building people, empowering them, and making them happy employees. Also, his volunteer leadership in the community was outstanding. He was promoted, then further promoted, until he became the corporate vice president for human resources.

His life had turned around. He finally found fulfillment in life. He also found a new freedom from the constraints of the denominationally-prescribed lifestyle he'd had years back while still serving the church. He became a happy, ethical person with noble values, but no longer religious.

Then one day, a couple days before he was to take his getaway break to Rio de Janiero, he received an invitation card to a leadership dinner. He went, but he hadn't expected it to be a Christian leadership dinner. Despite feeling uneasy, he tried to get along with others.

Unexpectedly, he met a lovely lady that caught his interest. The lady was sharing with him her life's journey, and he was impressed. He tried hiding his previous pastoral background and conversing with her as if he didn't know much about Christian faith at all, but slowly the lady's testimony seeped deeper into his heart.

He excused himself halfway through dinner and exchanged business cards before leaving. The thought of her and the little seeds of faith sprinkled on his heart were like a refreshing rain that quenched a drought-stricken land.

He went to Rio de Janeiro to enjoy the Carnival, but was instead drawn to the mountain of Corcovado.

He reflected ...

What a waste of time and money, preparing for pastoral ministry when I ended up happy and fulfilled in another career. Was it really God's will for me to shift from medicine to theology, then from theology to human resources?

Although I'm happy and fulfilled now, I could have been happier and more fulfilled earlier in life had it not been for my delusion of serving God and laying aside my medical career. Was it really God's will, or simply my own impression? I don't think God called me to be a pastor or theologian when I ended up losing those and becoming a successful human resources executive.

Well, whatever it is, if there's still you guiding my life and calling me to a particular vocation, just fulfill it ...

After talking to the God he'd missed for so long, he felt the unresolved animosity that had been lying dormant deep in his soul dissipate, and an overwhelming sense of peace engulfed him.

With a mind so serene and fertile for divine enlightenment, he smiled and said, "I know what you have called me for: to make the best of my life and seek happiness and fulfillment in the good life I choose, and to spread that happiness and a sense of fulfillment to others around me. Now I know the purpose of my life. It's not about my career. It's about making a good use of my life." He beamed, so happy with the newfound answer and fresh outlook on life.

He also imagined having a happy family with the lady he'd met at dinner.

"Wow! It looks like life is good after all."

He gleamed with enthusiasm for the good life ahead.

Where life
is no longer purposeless

The purpose of our life is to perpetuate …

"Wow! I can't believe it! I'm now at the earliest identified Christian house church." Luis was awed, looking intently inch-by-inch at the Dura-Europos house church.

The church was built around 235 AD, just about two centuries after the days of the apostles. Staring at the most ancient Christian painting at the most ancient baptistery—the reddish brownish frescoes of the "Good Shepherd," the healing of the paralytic, and Christ and Peter walking on the water—made him nostalgic of what it had have been like living in the time of Jesus, hearing him preach, seeing him do miracles, and literally following him every day.

Becoming aware that what he was seeing were relics of the past, he became even more reflective of what life really was.

After seeing the house church and taking some pictures, he strolled around the site and found a spot overlooking a lake. There, he sat down and reflected ...

"Life. What's it all about?" he asked himself, surrounded by the ruins of past civilization.

Then Luis took out the small photo album he brought on the trip in case he got bored on the plane. He looked at the pictures of when he was a crawling infant, then a curious kid, a young teen, a restless adolescent, and an adventurous young professional. All that was left of his childhood days were memories. He smiled and laughed, amused and nostalgic with years gone by.

He imagined his childhood days, the funny things he did, the carefree spirit he'd had. He'd pondered nothing about the future and life then. His parents were then young, busy earning money for their daily bread and saving money for their future and his education. Then he went to school. Oh, how he had loved his carefree elementary days. He was amused by his curious high school days. He smiled at his naïve college days. He recollected the challenges of his graduate school days.

Now his parents were gone. He was in his late fifties. All that was left of his old world were memories. The time would soon come when he would be gone from this world also. His only child was already grown up and had his own family. And his son would soon have his own children as well, and they, too, would get older and pass away.

"Is life just like that? A dream?" he asked. Then he reflected ...

I may acquire vast wealth, build a grand house, or even leave an impressive legacy, but I still have to accept the reality that though those things may hang around for a while, my life will fade away into the realm of memories.

Even if I make use of my time well and make breakthroughs in life, I will still be like a character in a dream. The time will come when the dream fades away.

Even yesterday, the minute or the seconds that ticked by are already moments that have faded out. Every tick of the clock is a moment ebbing away, and life is getting shorter and shorter. At the end of the day, and day after day, segments of my life are vanishing. And for all I know, I'll be reaching the limit of my life, either natural or unexpected. The good deeds I have done may linger for some time in some people's hearts. So will their memories of me. But my personal existence will vanish.

He further asked, "What, really, is the meaning of life? There must be more to life than its brevity. But what is it? Where are the true and lasting treasures of life?"

Glancing again at the empty ruins, sensing something grand, yet non-material, he sought the meaning of life in the inner sanctum of his being. He realized that the existence of life is a derived existence.

He continued reflecting ...

My life is endowed. I don't exist by my own self, and I don't and can't live by my own powers. I didn't originate my life, nor can I make it meaningful by myself. I was created by God and remain His creature. My life is derived from Him, and my existence depends upon Him. Even the very characteristic of my being is the image of him.

I'm nobody because I'm just a creature, but I am somebody because I'm the image of the Creator-God. It inspires in me the sanctity of my being. My life is sacred, and I exist for something more noble than the mere competition to survive or an obsession to ever have more.

My link with the God of creation engenders creative hope in my life. Hope is a powerful drive in human life, for hope engenders faith. Faith engenders optimism. Optimism engenders meaning in life.

But what does it mean to be a creature of God? Does it mean that life isn't short and that human life doesn't just fade away? Could human life indeed be eternal in the sense that my birth and existence is inherently linked to the neverending time of God?

Wow! Could aging really not be a process of decay, nor death the end of life, but part of the metamorphosis of life eternal? A metamorphosis from being a caterpillar in the cocoon of a transitory Earth, crawling amid the hardships of Earthly life, to being a butterfly in the garden of the eternal cosmos, nurturing while enjoying the beauty and wonders of life everlasting? As the universe is infinite, so is life.

Now I see! The nostalgia and loneliness of aging and death are nothing but mere emotional transitions from life ephemeral to life eternal.

But what about the frustrations, hardships, and all the pains of life on Earth?

Yeah, these are realities that I need to accept with a courageous spirit that soars beyond the transitory nature of this Earthly life while treasuring the new life yonder.

But shall I just live every day in mere anticipation of what's yonder?

He continued pondering ...

No, I don't think so.

For life in the present, being part of life in the hereafter, belongs to the wholeness of life. Like the stream of water flowing through a long and winding river in a rain forest, life continuously flows and carries with it either the purity of nature or the filthiness of humanity. The purity of heart, the happiness of daily life, and the wisdom of coping with life on Earth will be carried over as precious jewels in life henceforth. So are heartaches, disappointments, greed, and cruelties as defilements.

So now, what's the purpose of my life?

Now I see!

The purpose of my life is to perpetuate the creative nature of my life and existence. As God is the creator, I, too, am a creator-creature. I am created to be a divine creator to carry on the bliss from here to the hereafter. I have to be naturally creative in finding bliss in my present everyday life so I can be part of the everlasting, creative flow of life.

So I live and exist to enjoy the life I now have. I have to creatively cope with it and shape it toward a life of pure delight and fulfillment. I have to nurture and make use of the values of courage, hope, kindness, love, wisdom, and common good to creatively cope with life.

I have to envision and be passionate about a life that propagates reciprocal happiness and fulfillment among my fellow human beings. To do things for myself alone would be destruc-

146

tive and mar my pleasure of life in the present and in the here-after. To be engrossed in selfish insatiability would make my soul restless, entrench me in fleeting moments of delusion, and make me miss the much larger and more profound lasting joys in the wholeness of life.

Looking at the ruins, he imagined a community of people living harmoniously according to the creative values in life. He smiled.

"Paradise!" he said.

Epilogue of the Travelogues

Human life is an exciting journey, but full of ironies.

To be entrenched in a particular moment is to be stuck in the denial of life's incessancy. To always be restless and not find a home along one's journey is a rejection of the fulfillment that life offers to everyone.

To live a life so Heavenly, rejecting the pleasures of the Earthly, is a denial of the reality of the present. To live a life so Earthly, insatiably heaping up as many artifacts as we can exploit from our fellow human beings and nature, is a denial of the reality that life is both material and non-material.

We need to affirm and live in harmony with the continuity of the present and the future, the balance of the material and non-material. For life is not a fragment of time, nor a share of artifacts. It's a universal system of reciprocal existence with all that exists interconnected with one another to bring the beauty and wonder of life to our otherwise vast but void and lifeless universe.

We are all one, and no one is all. When one tries to become all, one has not only destroyed oneself, but also others. When everyone is engrossed in the varied fragments of life, we all cause the disintegration of our shared life. For life is like a rainbow with varied colors, but together as one, it becomes colorful and beautiful. Separated, it no longer becomes a beautiful rainbow, but a weird, if not eerie, ray.

So is faith!

For centuries, Christians have become accustomed to fragmenting faith. Faith either means a denominational set of beliefs that contradict one another, an assumed exclusive right to a universal Creator-Savior-God and the Heaven He offers, or a belief in a particular denomination as the preferred, if not the only, gateway to the Heavenly hereafter.

Each group of opposing devotees dedicates their lives, money, and future to their respective religious organizations, and faith has become institutionalized. But it seems that faith cannot but always be institutional. With its institutionalization comes the exploitation and commercialization of conscience.

But could there be faith, pure essence of Christian faith, beyond sectarian enclosures? Faith that's in profound harmony with the ancient teachings of Christ, yet transcends traditional notions?

The irony is: yes and no. Yes, for faith in God is ideally personal. No, for faith in God generally can no longer be detached from a particular community of devotees. Miracles for Pentecostals, the gospel for evangelicals, rituals for Catholics and Orthodox, etc. A life of faith has become a church brand. The faithful are the faithful Catholics, the faithful Protestants, the faithful Pentecostals, the faithful Orthodox, etc.

Christ has become a Catholic Christ, a Protestant Christ, a Pentecostal Christ, an Orthodox Christ. Superficial rapprochement has been tried, but candidly deep in everyone's soul is a rooted conviction in one's own church brand.

Can Christians transcend their dogged segregationist spirits? For now, I don't think so.

Am I concluding this book with a critique of the Christian faith? Yes and no. Yes, because I wish to put faith in the context of one's personal journey in life. No, because this book is not merely about institutional criticism or theological discussion on who's right or wrong.

This book is about the essence of the Christian faith that spiritually binds Christians together despite their superficial diversity. Faith is about our personal journey with God. It's not about our conflicting organizations. Faith is

150

deeply spiritual, and spirit transcends material boundaries. It seeps through one's soul, transforms individual lives, enables us to cope with the seemingly insurmountable odds of present, everyday life, and empowers us to shape a bright yonder.

We can only serenely smile amid adversities
when our eyes open to a fresh vision
that gives us purpose in life.

This world is so beautiful,
that to insist seeing it only in one color
is a degradation of its beauty and wonders.

The Conversation

The Divine Rendezvous

Two men, one with a seven-year-old son, and a woman instinctively converged in a Starbucks Coffee in the lobby of the Sheraton on the Falls in Niagara.

After sipping his cup of coffee, one of the men laid his book face down on the table, and asked the man with the child, "What do you have there?"

"Oh, Dawkins' *God Delusion*," the man shyly answered. "What about you?"

"Hmm, C.S. Lewis' *Mere Christianity*," also answering shyly. "By the way, I'm Leith."

"I'm Krister, and this is my son, JK."

"Hi!" JK greeted, waving his hand.

"Gentlemen, may I join you?" a gorgeous lady in her mid-thirties asked.

"Sure!" the men answered at the same time with the warmth of instant friendship, as though they had known one another for a long time.

"I'm Elise." The lady offered her right hand for a handshake while holding in the other a cup of coffee whose aroma added enchantment to the ambiance.

"I'm Krister, and this is my son JK," Krister said, shaking Elise's hands with a warm smile.

"And I'm Leith," said the other man cordially, shaking Elise's hands with sweet smile and captivating look.

JK stood and pulled the chair for Elise. "Have a seat, ma'am."

"Thank you! You're such a lovely boy."

"You're welcome." JK gestured like a matador welcoming a bull to his cloak.

"Look what I've got," Elise said, showing her audio book. "It's a *Wayne Dyer's Audio Collection*. And what do you guys have?"

"It's interesting, we've all got something religious," Leith replied. "I have something Christian, Krister has something about atheism, and you've got something spiritual."

"Are you a Christian?" Elise asked Leith.

"Not really," he replied.

"What about you, Krister, are you an atheist?"

157

"Not really," Krister answered.

"And what about you? Are you into something spiritual?" Krister asked Elise.

"Not really either," Elise answered with a smile, repeating what the two guys said.

JK reacted: "Hello, guys, it looks like you're all not sure of yourselves."

They laughed, but the boy's comment echoed deep in their hearts. They stared at him for a moment, everyone telling him in thought, 'You're right, boy, you're right.'

JK understood their actuation and replied, "Okay guys, if you want to be sure about yourselves, why don't you talk about God? Isn't God the only sure thing in this world?"

JK's comment deeply touched their hearts again, this time with something more poignant. While staring at JK again, everyone remembered the turning points in their lives.

~

KRISTER reminisced about when his mom had been in a coma and dying. A couple of months ago, his dad had unexpectedly passed away also. The busyness of everyday life had made him forever lose the precious heart-to-heart talks he used to have with his dad. Suddenly, he was faced with losing those precious moments again with his mom.

Beside her bed, he pleaded in tears for God's miracle. But his mom's condition was just getting worse and worse. The doctor tried to revive her whenever her heartbeat began slipping, but on the third day the doctor told him that his mom's case was hopeless; only a miracle could save her. The more he pleaded with God, the more he shed tears for God's failed promises.

Disappointment with the God he worshipped, worsened by days of sleepless nights and missed meals, was dragging his spirit into the abyss of gloom. It made his body feeble so that he felt he could no longer persevere in prayer. The more his mom's heartbeat faded, the more kindling was applied to the pain in his soul.

"Sir, what shall we do next time her heartbeat goes down? the attending doctor asked. "The cardiologist already told you of her condition."

He sobbed. "Just do whatever you think is best," he replied, with the foreboding of what would happen, without consenting to end medical intervention.

The evening came and he went home. He gathered his last strength to pray, and all he could say was, "Please God ..." Then he realized that instead of pleading for miracles, he needed to entrust her into God's heavenly care. He did. And the images of *Revelation's* New Jerusalem flashed into his mind and he saw himself hugging his mom and his dad with tears of joyful reunion.

"Thank you God for reminding me that I can still see my mom and my dad again. When that day comes, I'll spend every day conversing with them and letting them know how much I loved them. I'll tell them how very sorry I was for not spending time with them when they needed me most. Bye for now, Dad, Mom. I'll see you again. I'll see you again ..." Then he fell sound asleep as never before.

Refreshed, and with a trustful spirit, he awoke in the morning with a beaming soul. "Good morning, Heavenly Father, from this day onward I'll entrust everything into your hands. Never shall I relegate you to the fringes of my life again." He spoke to God like a long lost friend he visited amid his solitude.

LEITH recollected how he had finally bid farewell to his once-cherished faith. Between one experience and another, Leith was left doubting the divine authenticity of religion. The pressures of doubts and critical-mindedness, compounded by the predicaments of faith-claims, had been shaping him into a new breed of free and enlightened person.

"Finally, I'm free! I will no longer allow exploitation of my conscience!" he sighed with great relief, laying aside the sacred scriptures he valued for so long.

He realized his worship of God had promoted a long list of vanities. A few examples were:

- Political scheming in the church that was no different from dirty secular politics.
- Racial discrimination and segregation among churches avoided even by the worldly.
- Vicious war (Sunni Muslims against Shiite Muslims, Catholics against Protestants, and Protestants among themselves) and unrelenting cold war (believers among themselves) perpetrated in honor of a sublime God.
- Moneymaking that outdid even greedy corporations.
- And mundane commercialization of heavenly paradise.

If the followers of religions were who they claimed to be, they could have lived more altruistic and helpful lives. If the God they worshiped were real, he could have transformed his worshipers into a new breed of noble human species. However, they were no different from anybody else. Why? Because there's no difference between folk superstition, the ancient worship of emperors, humanistic philosophy, and present religions. They're all alike—handiwork of people wanting to exploit and control the conscience of those with weak psyches, he realized.

"This day onward, I'll have nothing to do with religion anymore ..."

ELISE recalled the days of her serious depression. She had been so dismayed that she was weary with welcoming every morning as a new day. Often she shivered thinking that she, once daddy's lovely and smart girl, would break the heart of the father she loved so dearly.

Three times she thought of ending her life. But imagining the father she loved so dearly, though no longer in this world, grieving the loss of his adored darling, enabled her to transcend such senselessness. She tried her best in each of her three marriages, but they just didn't work. She had done all that she could, but they all left her.

She sought the help of pastors, but they offered her nothing more than an illusion of divine intervention. She consulted professional counselors, but they offered her conflicting advice. She called friends and they expressed regrets, but were busy coping with their own challenges.

"Was it me? Was it them? Or is it just the way life in this world is?" she asked.

To find peace in her soul, she sought answer in Christian faith. But confused by the many competing brands of Christianity, all claiming to be the exclusive franchisee of God and heaven, she fled Christianity like a plague. Then she tried other religions and only became more confused. But while searching and not finding the answer, surprisingly, something bright and beautiful was blossoming in her soul. She found new enthusiasm in life, and her depression began to wane, until she found herself no longer hurting.

"Who cares anyway? I'll just live my life one day at a time. Whatever makes me happy and soothes my soul, I'll take hold of it. Whatever doesn't, I'll just let go," she said. "Dad, your darling will stand on her feet again—bold and blithe." She smiled and imagined her dad hugging her and whispering the inspiring words, "You did it, my dear! And I'm proud of you."

Realizing that nothing in life is certain and that she still had a life to live after all, she hummed Ray Evans' song *Que sera sera, whatever will be will be* ... " Whatever my fate brings me, I'll accept with thankfulness and serenity. Nothing in this world is certain anyway. It'll all change, if not fade away. Life is a constant flux. I just have to find quietness while enjoying it ..."

Surprisingly, JK's invitation to talk about God gave everyone a new impetus. They were all thrilled to share their newfound perspectives on life. No one had expected that their seemingly trivial coffee talk could lead to something profound, or that the child's nuggets of wisdom would launch them to moving journeys they hadn't imagined before.

The Mundane Melting Pot

"Okay, let's talk about something that displeases me, yet, ironically, something that I'm enthusiastic talking about," said Leith.

"Oh! Oh! You mean …? My goodness! That's sacrilege, my friend, that's sacrilege," Krister replied.

"It's not, my friend," Elise reacted. "What's sacrilegious about something that you're not even sure exists?"

Krister responded: "You mean God does not exist? Look at the world around you, gaze at the expanse of the starry sky at night and see how vast this universe is, yet it's orderly. Look at nature, its design, its wonders, how a seed will grow into a tree. Nature speaks about our loving God who created the universe. Don't you guys realize that?"

"I know this is a revered matter for believers," said Leith, "while a laughing stock for the secular. So, before we converse about something as delicate as this, let's make a deal to discuss it with intellectual maturity and open-mindedness. Let's allow each other to speak freely according to one's convictions, reason, and experiences without prejudice.

Elise said: "How pleasing would our friendship be when we sincerely listened to one another as fellows in a coffee shop and in the world we live? Who knows, this conversation could be life-changing for us all. We could have a divine rendezvous rippling through our lives. What do you guys think?"

"Sorry if I'm a bit impulsive," replied Krister.

"No problem, my friend," Elise responded, while standing and motioning to hug. Krister stood also. "Here's to my dear Krister, ahhh!" Then she motioned to hug Leith. Leith stood. "And to you also Leith, ahhh! Is it warm enough to make us all cordial yet candid colleagues?" They were all smiles, charmed by Elise. A warmhearted friendship was blossoming among them. And they felt connected, like pieces of a jigsaw puzzle that were about to portray a grand mosaic of faith.

A journalist, doing research on coffee shop conversations, was snooping on the trio's conversation on his high-definition listener, and he thought:

BUT ... is it possible for three people, each with varied worldviews, to listen sincerely to one another and still be friends? Even in our society today, where we value freedom of religion as one of our important social principles, believers and atheists still consider each other mortal enemies. Ironically, though, atheists and agnostics can associate with each other with more respect than believers among themselves.

In politics, people change parties. In faith, people die for it. I can't understand how religious sectarianism became so ingrained in people's psyches when they all regard the God they worship as universal. Religious people even regard attending each other's churches as heresy punishable by expulsion from membership.

Now what have we here: a believer listening to both atheist and agnostic? Gosh! I couldn't imagine how his church would react. And what about an atheist listening to a believer? How would his fellow atheists react? Will they feel that he's falling back into superstition?

Why don't they just accept that they enrich one another's lives, and recognize that no human being is an island? Life is an interconnected and interacting system. Why can't they see one another as part of one universal worldview that enriches human life? Why can't they, as civilized human beings, just be cordially harmonious instead of thinking narrowly and separating one another?

167

"May I start then?" Leith asked.

"Sure!" Krister answered.

"Let me expound on why I don't believe in God," Leith said.

"Oh no, looks like this is gonna be serious," JK reacted. "Hope you guys will still be friends after this. Dad, can I watch my movie now?" The guys smiled.

"Sure!" Krister replied.

"And what's that movie?" Elise asked.

"It's my favorite, *Evan Almighty*. I watched it before, but I'd like to watch it again. I love this movie. It's so funny. And I couldn't believe that God likes to have fun too. He makes Evan save the world in a funny way. But why can't God just stay with Evan all the time? Why does he appear, then disappear, and appear again? And why do people have to wear a long beard when they're saving the world? Anyway, may I watch my movie now?" JK said, putting on his 72-inch 3-D iWear.

JK's witty thoughts amused the guys.

"Okay, let's listen to Leith, now," Elise said, and then she added, "It looks like this will be the most exciting coffee talk I've ever had."

If not for faith,
what else have we as an anchor in life?

*Haven't you realized that religion
is merely a metaphor for human wishes?*

Why I don't believe in God

Part I

hy don't I believe in God? Because when we are perceptive enough to see the realities behind religion, we realize that, indeed, there is no God, except the gods religions created according to their conflicting images. Now, let me point out the reasons that made me realize that God is nothing but a mere human creation who does not exist.

First, there is a lack of coherent universal management of human life by an all-knowing, all-powerful, and all-present being whom believers call God. Let me share with you this news I downloaded from GlobalIssues.org.

Leith took the note he inserted in Lewis' book and read:

Today, over 22,000 children died around the world by Anup Shah. Last Updated Monday, September 20, 2010 Over 22,000 children die every day around the world. That is equivalent to:

1 child dying every 4 seconds.

15 children dying every minute.

A 2010 Haiti Earthquake occurring almost every 10 days.

A 2004 Asian Tsunami occurring almost every 10 days.

An Iraq-scale death toll every 18-43 days.

Just under 8.1 million children dying every year.

Some 88 million children dying between 2000 and 2009.

The silent killers are poverty, hunger, easily preventable diseases and illnesses, and other related causes.

Now, I have two crucial questions here. First, amid all these sufferings, where are the rich God-worshiping countries? Is God deficient in power to transform his worshipers into altruistic people? Look how extravagant the rich Middle Eastern Muslim countries are, while the rest of their fellow Muslims are destitute and hungry. The money they spend on lavish buildings and lifestyles could improve the lives of millions of deprived Muslims. Look also at the wastefulness of many Christian Western countries while the rest of their fellow Christians are living in abject poverty.

If God has the power to change lives, and the worship of God is life-transforming, his worshipers could live a more modest life, then significantly share what they have to equalize the dignity of human life. But see who are the exploiters and hoarders of the world's natural resources and wealth. Are they not all God-worshipers?

And *also*, the major predicament in believing in God: where is God amid the deaths of these innocent helpless and hopeless children? What about the millions who lose their lives as victims of human brutalities and natural disasters?

"But this is part of the mystery," Krister interrupted.

"Krister, no interrupting, please," Elise quickly responded.

"Please go on, Leith," she added.

If there is a God, where is he amid all this global wretchedness? Believers are ever-ready to defend God. Many of them would even argue that God's absence amid tragedies is part of the divine mystery. If so, then why is God hiding from the accountability that defines his tender loving kindness and being the Creator-God and Savior of Humanity? Is it a part of the mystery of God, or merely an excuse of believers to hide the blindness of their beliefs?

I have yet to be a father, but imagine this scenario: People know you as a wealthy and loving father. One day, your beloved child is in the street shivering in the cold, sick and hungry, begging for food and help to everyone who passes by. But they all ignore him as if he were a social outcast. And you pass by in your limousine, glance at him and say, "I love you, my son." Then you just leave him on the street to suffer till death. Somebody asks, "Why did he not save his beloved son?" Those who adore you as a wealthy and loving father answer, "That's all part of the mystery of the father's love."

Elise smiled. Krister was silent.

What a ridiculous proposition! No father who loves his child can do that. Even if he is not the father of that child, any normal human being will naturally sympathize with a child shivering in the cold, sick and hungry. Passerbys will usually call for help to save a child's life. Where was God when millions of his children were shivering in cold, if not scorched by the sun, sick, hungry and dying?

Some amusing guys even guessed that after creating the universe, he just left everything in our hands. Others say he's always there, but what is he doing? Just watching his beloved creations suffer and die? Doing nothing, just like the fictitious dad in the limousine? Then it's inconsis-

174

tent with the belief that God loves and cares for his valued human creatures.

And please don't tell me it's because of Adam. What if your great-great-grandfather committed a crime? For instance, stole an apple from a neighbor's farm because, coming from the tropics, he was curious about how a North American apple would taste. So the state sentenced him with hard labor everyday of his life till death.

Then, after sentencing him, the state also declared an endless sentence to all his progeny. That includes you and your son and your grandchildren. Do you think this is rational and just? But that's exactly what Christianity teaches. And what's ironic is that this is also inconsistent with the belief that God is just. You see, the Christian concept of original sin is as dehumanizing as the Hindu belief in the untouchables.

Or let's portray another scenario. Probably, believers still need to plead earnestly in prayer, so God could finally be compassionate to the destitute. But I bet, even if all believers in the world would pray every day for blooming crops in the arid African desert, the ending of calamities, and equally restoring the dignity of human life, still nothing would happen. Why? Because believers are just fantasizing about the existence of God. God is merely a psychological tool they created so they could have an imaginary anchor in life that they otherwise couldn't find in the reality of every day.

Elise reacted: "Hmmm, you've got a point there, Leith. God as a psychological anchor?" Leith also realized that Krister had said something that touched his soul.

Second, as I have already alluded to, the absence of divine interventions in human life in particular, and the natural world in general. Even if God is not managing his universal creation 24/7, at least he could have intervened in overwhelming human-made and natural disasters.

Look, for instance, at the catastrophes of the early part of the Twentieth Century. An estimated sixteen million people died in the First World War, excluding the twenty-one million wounded. You know how many died in the 1918 flu pandemic? About fifty million! That's three percent of the then estimated 1.6 billion world population. And the infection spread to a whopping five hundred million, or one-third of the world's population at that time.

Were there divine interventions? None! Or probably the death toll wasn't enough yet to awaken the slumbering God. Or perhaps, as in the story of Noah, he just wanted to destroy the world so he could repopulate it with a new generation of human beings worshiping only one God. And whose God would that be: the Protestant, the Catholic, the Pentecostal, the Muslim, the Hindu God? What a merciless proposition then!

If the death tolls I mentioned were not enough, what about the sixty million more casualties in World War II? What about the wanton injustice and cruelty to six million Jews? Weren't the Jews regarded as God's chosen people in the Old Testament? Where was he when the inhuman Hitler was slaughtering the Jews? Abandoning them as he did with the millions and millions of his other beloved human creatures? What about the more than 220,000 deaths in the 2010 Haiti Earthquakes? The 230,000 dead in the 2004 Asian tsunami? And the more than 800,000 (an average of 10,000 per day) Tutsis killed by Hutu Militia in Rwanda? And many more from both natural and human-made calamities?

Is God incapable of preventing disaster? Is he power-less to end human cruelties? Or did he allow it simply be-cause human beings chose to sin against him? I bet be-lievers, at times, would even rejoice in the tragedy of others not belonging to their religious clan. They would claim tragedy to others as God's judgment for not believing in their particular notion of faith.

But the truth is, there is no divine intervention because there is no God at all. If there is an omnipotent God who created the universe by merely saying a word, why could he not declare, "Let there be no more natural and human-made disasters." It won't take him a minute or two of his infinite time to do that. It's as simple as that. The truth is, belief in God offers nothing more than a temporary and illusory solace for the bereaved. Practical and more realistic grief counseling can do better than this illusion.

Third, defects in nature reveal there is no perfect and all-knowing designer as believers assumed. Aside from the many flaws of human and animal anatomies, look also at the way humans and animals survive. Most animals survive by being predators to one another. What kind of designer is that, who designs his creatures to live by killing one another? And don't tell me it's all about original sin again.

What do you think a conscientious architect does when he finds a flaw in his cherished projects? Just pursue his projects as they are and endanger people's lives? Even sensible human beings correct the defects in their valued projects, but why not God? It doesn't make sense for an omniscient and loving Creator to neglect the predatory nature of the creatures he designed and cherished. It's not fun to see divine creatures, human beings and animals alike, killing and foraging one another just to survive.

Well, believers say, God created everything perfect in the Garden of Eden. But who knew about what was going on then? Most believers, of course, assume the Bible came fresh as God handed it to Moses, and as fresh today as it was thousands of years ago. I wish their scholars and educated clergy would just be honest enough to tell their adherents the truth about the Bible. The Bible was the product of compiling ancient manuscripts, each with thousands of variations. And ancient publishers recopied these manuscripts countless times by hand in the bygone era before photocopying was invented.

Those who chose which manuscripts to include in the Bible were not angels, but people with preconceived notions of what they thought God should think like. They even discarded, if not destroyed, many other ancient writings that did not fit into their mindsets. Besides, how could we regard the Old Testament writings as the actual account of the origin of the universe when the Hebrew language and literature emerged much later in history? And where now was that Garden of Eden so believers could see the prototype of perfect creation? In fact, many Jewish Rabbis regard the stories of the Old Testament as allegories of spiritual matters rather than literal history.

Now, back to our imperfect human nature. Imagine the God who loves life, creating human beings who subsist by slaughtering, every day, billions and billions of their fellow creatures. Do these animals feel pain too? Do they also mourn the loss of their beloved families? Of course! But what can we do? That's all part of our imperfect existence that thrives on the survival of the most powerful. Had there been a perfect Creator-God, it couldn't have been so. Some people even recommend vegetarianism as a more humane way to subsist. But is there enough balanced vegetation to feed us all? Besides, not all species of fruits and vegetables grow in one place.

And another point, what's the purpose of making some places harshly cold and others severely hot, and not all conducive to human, animal, and plant life? If I were to design the Earth as a normal rational man, I would make its entire topography livable for all life. Designing one place as fertile and another as harsh could result in both an imbalanced ecosystem and inequitable quality of life.

Well, believers would argue that God originally created the Earth perfect, but because human beings were evil, God brought floods to destroy the Earth and human and animal lives, including plants. Could you bear seeing hundreds of thousands of innocent children drowning because their parents did something bad? What loving Creator-God would do that? And not only drowning them, but also en-suring the next generation will live on an even harsher planet filled with dangerous precipices and treacherous weather?

Even our penal institutions provide for rehabilitation. Declaring the regenerating word, "transform," is much easier and more humane than forty days of flood that didn't transform humanity at all. Even the Bible itself tells us that after the flood human beings became evil again. So God's plan, with all his omniscience, did fail after all.

Consider another grave flaw—harshness of nature that threatens our life beyond control. If we were the crowning works of God, he should have given us natural powers to manage the destructive forces of nature. Or just take destructive forces out of nature. Well, you may say, our natural disasters are human-made, resulting from misdirected industrial culture that has abused nature. Yes, we have abused nature and brought curses of disasters on ourselves. But what about natural disasters long before there was an industrial revolution, like Noah's flood, if you believe it to be true?

The truth is, the stories of the Bible are nothing more than ancient myths that þelievers blindly assume to be real. Although the Bible contains some spiritual lessons, their stories are not historical facts. Besides, there were several other ancient writings also. But when Constantine institutionalized Christianity in 325 AD, the church leaders he commissioned to collect ancient writings deified some and nullified others. The deified collection is what we now call the Bible. Of course, the Jews considered the Old Testament as sacred because it speaks about their hopes. Just as the Vedas speak for Hindus, the Tao Te Ching and Analects for Chinese, and the Kojiki for the Japanese. But to adore a particular ancient writing as *the* account of the origin of the universe is nothing but a myth. When one talks about God, either in the ancient or the present sense, it's all about myths that are symbolic expressions of human yearnings.

Another painful design flaw—the pangs of birth. If I were to design the female human and animal species, I would design them in such a way that birth would be more exhilarating than sexual orgasm. So giving birth to a new human being brings together emotions of exploding joy and a deep sense of fulfillment to celebrate life.

"Phew! That would be great!" Elise reacted, jesting, but suddenly turning a bit somber, recalling her miseries of losing stillborn babies on two occasions. "You're right, Leith, nature is defective. In fact, it's also an abortionist," she silently said to herself.

"Are you okay, Elise?" Krister asked.

"Oh, sorry, yah!" Elise replied. "Go on Leith," she said.

Why let the female species suffer pain while bringing new life on Earth? Should we not welcome life with joy instead of pain? And don't tell me it's because God punished Eve. It's sadistic to assume that. Or don't tell me it was the result of eating a forbidden fruit. Even if the fruit poisoned Eve, where was God's power of damage-control? Or why, as the sole creator, create humans in such a way that you foresee them suffering? Why didn't he ensure the safety and bliss of his beloved creatures?

Think of an engineer creating a bridge that he foresaw seriously collapsing and resulting in many deaths and sufferings. Or think of loving parents who have a choice to deliver and raise a child in a safe and healthy environment, but who bring their much-loved child to the worst ravaged war zone to abandon him.

Before abandoning him, they leave a note for him to read when he grows up, reading, "We have put you in a war-torn homeland. We are giving you the freedom to choose which band to follow. Choose wisely. If you choose the wrong group, we will come again to punish you. Now live and survive: Your loving parents." This is pure nonsense. I wish believers could realize how absurd their theology of God and their belief in the origin of the human species are.

183

Even normal human beings can do better than the God characterized by religions. For instance, when an inventor creates something and he sees defects, he doesn't just throw it away. He corrects the defects to make it better, and thus fulfills the purpose he intended for it. Throwing away his handiwork is not just a tantrum, but also like throwing away his being an inventor, because it's part of him and it defines who he is.

Think of the many inventions we have that brought efficiency and comfort to our lives, complementing our natural human abilities. If inventors followed the manner of the God characterized by religions, imagine the results of every error inventors commit. The world would be full of abandoned, defective creations. And punishment would await inventors for every error they commit while exploring breakthroughs for bettering human life, as in the story of Eve who was just curious to know more.

"But can human beings create?" Krister interrupted.

"Krister," Elise reminded.

"Oh, sorry, again," Krister replied.

I know what you'd like to say. "Can human beings create human beings?" Of course! We mate, and that's a part of our natural procreative power. But if there is a God, he could have prepared a perfect planet on which every human being could live, so every time we reproduced we would welcome a new human being into a perfect home. But how many millions of innocent newborn babies, aside from the toddlers, the teens, and the grownups, die every year because of our defective home-planet and defective lives we lead?

Both natural and human-made calamities haunt us. He doesn't need to sweat it out. All he needs to do is just say a few words in a few seconds: "Regenerate into perfection!" And bingo! He could save billions of sacred, precious lives, and we would all have new wholesome lives on a suitable and safe home-planet. But the truth is, the Creator-God that religions portray is nonexistent and merely a mythological being.

Fourth, we cannot confine the cosmic reality of our human understanding. Religious claims about God and creation are claims about realities beyond humanity. How can we ever fully grasp realities that are beyond the limit of our senses and thoughts?

Think, for instance, of five ants in a Grand Canyon colony proclaiming varied revelations about human beings. One even claims elevation to human status. Each of them promotes their own human revelations. Another describes human beings as the fastest quadruped with a sense of smell greater than all of them combined. And another says human beings created the first and largest queen ant ever with the most virile male ant. Then the human creator placed the first ant couple in the best colony ever, filled with all sorts of human crumbs. So, everyday ants need to worship human beings by biting them hard when ants meet them, so they will bring more crumbs. This may sound sensible for ants because this portrayal reflects their longings and patterns of life.

Religion is like this. It's nothing but a portrayal of human yearnings and archetypes of human life. It's just an attribution of human forms to the ideals of superhuman beings, utopia, and how to reach utopia. How could ants ever understand human reality? They don't have a clue about careers, rising and falling realty prices, money, or technology. These are all beyond ant-life realities and sense experiences. Look at the vastness of the cosmos. If indeed there is an originator of all realities, that reality is not human, nor can we fully explain it in human terms.

Yes, believers find comfort and hope in religion, but it's just that, a psychological tool they create to help them cope with the realities of life. In fact, religion is not even as realistic as other prac-tical-oriented motivational approaches, because it always promotes a mystical and illusory way of coping with life.

Further, think about the religious characterization of God as male. What about God as female? Have you not realized that if our human characterization of God is true, what we have is a Creator-God who is like us? He would also have sexual organs and sexual needs, digestive and excretory organs, and so on, otherwise his body would be useless. Did God create human beings according to his image? Or is it human beings who created God according to their images?

Often religion uses its portrayal of God to manipulate people's conscience. We always hear self-claimed spokesmen declaring their wishes, however exploitive or cruel these are, as God's will. And indoctrinated believers blindly follow what they assume to be divine declarations because of fear that disobedience will bring eternal doom to their souls. But if we are just reasonable enough to listen to our sanity, we'll discover the truth about the origin of religion. It's nothing but someone's mystical theory after deep frustrations and depressions. Just look at the pattern of how the founders of religion started spreading their beliefs.

For example, Moses—if he were real—amid his frustration of the chaos and constant rebellion of his people, offered the Ten Commandments as a tool to bring order to his community. Did God write in Hebrew and in stone and speak in the Hebrew language to Moses? Or was the story simply an allegorical answer to social-spiritual needs?

Did Mary bear a son with God? Or was it a story that Constantine and the religious-political leaders institutionalized to promote the unity of beliefs intended to strengthen the unity of an empire? Did Jesus rise to heaven? People in ancient times thought that above the Earth was heaven, and the world was like a tier of three flat surfaces. They didn't realize, as we do today, that the Earth is just floating in vast space. Did an angel named Gabriel speak in Arabic to Mohamed? Did God tell a bedtime story in Hebrew to Moses on how he created the universe? Did God commission Jesus in Aramaic or Greek to die on a cross to save humanity?

Or like Buddha, after an intense period of frustration and seclusion, writers of so-called sacred literatures developed a new viewpoint. They realized what they wished for were ideals of life. They reached a heightened awareness about their dormant wishes regarding how human beings should live in contrast to what they regarded as dehumanizing social context. Then they were able to finally put into words the latent imagery they had been forming in their subconscious minds. Those words became the "divine messages" that followers call divine revelations.

Another point: if we take a critical look at the teachings of world religions, we discover they all include previous beliefs. They were innovations of earlier beliefs and practices. Founders and followers then turned their views into dogmas, created institutions out of them, set up societies, and amassed political influences with divine attribution, becoming recognized religions and powerful competing manipulators of people's consciences. Their power resided in people's conviction that religion holds the rights to the eventual destiny of the human soul and the universe. Religion is the greatest of all hoaxes in our civilization.

Despite the deception of religion, I won't deny that there are also some good teachings in religion, like the teaching of compassion and charity. And it can be noble as well, especially if serving as a practical tool to regenerate global society. Imagine its potential social impact of religion if it, instead of spreading destructive fanaticism and social segregation, zealously promoted a productive way of life.

"You're right, Leith. I'm also concerned about the dogged segregation of Christian churches. We look at each other not only as competitors but as mortal enemies. We can't give up our iron curtain because we think that when we become friends, we will lose our God. Our claim of the love of Jesus

189

can't bind us as Christ's one universal family of renewed people," Krister commented.

"Thank you for your candid remark," Leith replied.

"Have your coffee first, it looks like it's getting cold," Elise
said.

"Thanks," Leith answered.

A pause of silence followed, as if everyone were trying to
digest the hard stuff of candid conversation.

Why I don't believe in God
Part II

"Okay, let's keep the ball rolling," Elise said. Leith continued:

Fifth, there is an absence of the continuing revelation of God apart from ancient writings. Communication is basic in every relationship. How do you think JK would feel if you, being his dad, talked to him just once a year? Or, although you said you're with him every day, what if, when he wants to converse with you and ask for your help, you don't answer? His teacher asks him, "Does your dad talk for you?" He answers, "I believe he listens but he doesn't talk to me. He just left me a letter after birth, and I have to figure out what his answer will be for all my needs." Is this scenario sensible?

Then, what if he finds many other letters, every one claiming the truth and as the genuine letter of his father, but all conflict one another? He seeks clarification. And someone claims, "I am your father's best friend, and I have spent years studying his letters, and this is what he would like to tell you." Then he meets many other scholars also claiming to know his father and to have spent years of dogged research on his father's letter.

My goodness! Isn't this foolish? If your father were real, living, loving, and with you every day, couldn't he just talk to you? Of course! A real and loving father communicates with his child daily. And they always excitingly converse, and their communication is two-way, interactive, and personal. Even when one is away, they still communicate with each other through phone or internet.

Well, believers would naturally say that he's God, and not human like us. Besides, he left the Bible or Koran for us to know his will. If he is not human like us, then why do we think of him in human terms and regard our human thinking of him as unquestionable and final? If the Bible or the Koran is God's revelation, why didn't he, in all his omniscience, give us an unambiguous text so various human interpretations wouldn't confuse his clear message?

Look how Sunni and Shiite Muslims fight to death about who has the right interpretation of Allah's will.

Christians did that too in the past, and continue their cold war in the present. If the God they all adore is real, does he love watching his worshipers shedding blood, just to find out who among them is right about him?

God-believing religions have clearly been creating idols they can promote as rallying points to colonize others and spread their self-centered beliefs. They are offering collections of preconceived notions about what God, assuming he exists, would say to human beings, and nothing more than that. So with various religious founders doggedly presenting diverse speculations, they fill the world with many conflicting religions and vie for dominance.

Is there a personal Creator-God who runs the universe and tells us his will? And if so, what language is he using? It's too culturally biased if he only speaks either Hebrew or Arabic or Greek, and not even the Greek that most Greeks speak today. Why not English, Cantonese, Hindi, and other languages spoken by many people in the world? And why chat for a bit in the past then hide for centuries when we need him? If God is who he is, as religion portrays him, then he is a poor communicator.

Besides, why only leave ancient manuscripts to guide us through our lives, when our way of life is ever-changing? Life two thousand years ago differs from the present. There was then no genetic engineering offering recreative possibilities. No space explorations proving there are not three tiers of heaven, Earth and hell in our world. And no advanced medical science offering laboratory-made medicines that keep modern humans from solely depending on supernatural miracle to cure diseases.

If God is an all-knowing communicator, he could have devised means to communicate his message effectively and clearly, so believers wouldn't misinterpret it. And he should also update his message every time new realities emerge. A sensible CEO would always provide communication updates to employees. Why, if God is real and personal, can't he do it too?

Well, the only reason I can think of is that the religious claims of God are nothing but the products of ancient human reflections. Adherents then reformulated those ancient claims in diverse forms to suit what they variedly thought God should be. Because they had different personalities and concerns about life, they also created conflicting theories and reformulations about God and his will. Just think how confusing God-believing religions are. Not only are the general religious classifications contradicting one another, but also the many sects within each. Couldn't you just see what folly believers have created to confuse people susceptible to manipulation of conscience? In its truest sense, religion is not about God. It's about spreading one's particular wishes and fantasies in life, borne of deep frustrations. Essentially, religion is nothing but promoting an illusion of utopia amid hopelessness. And above all it's about taking control of people's consciences to manipulate them toward a selfish institutional end.

Sixth, it's undeniable that human reflection is the root of portraying God's will and identity. Was there an extra-terrestrial super-being called God, who can't even communicate with us today, but who conversed with Moses, Jesus, or Mohammed? At least some Eastern religions are more honest and less exploitive than Western religions in affirming that human reflection is the root of divine enlightenment. The historical authenticity of the founders of Western religions, except Islam, is still dubious, but let's look honestly and closely at the pattern of how Western religions started.

First you can see the founders' deep frustrations against tradition and what was going on in society. Then out of frustration, they secluded themselves—desert for Moses and Jesus, cave for Mohammed—and went into self-denial—suggesting depression. Finally, after days of intense contemplations, they emerged out of their seclusions with realizations of fresh worldviews. They then spread these worldviews as divine revelations.

195

Eventually, on their account of being the bearer of divine revelations, their followers anointed them as the chosen prophets of God. Or, as with Jesus, even God him-self. Afterward, when the founders were gone, followers began reflecting and developing their varied views, which suited their respective wishes and fantasies about their founder's teachings. The results are numerous religious sects that are in constant war with one another.

Ironically, what followers assumed as a new and divine way of life, also become the potent cause for dehumanizing others. When believers institutionalize their beliefs, it becomes not just a 'divine' worldview but also a mundane religion. With institutionalization comes the merger of authority to manipulate conscience and financial and political powers that stir compulsive colonization of others with differing religious beliefs. The results are religious-political wars that are more vicious than secular wars. Why? Because whether one lives to see victory or one dies to go to heaven, it doesn't matter anymore.

What's foolish is that zealots don't realize that all they're fighting for is merely a matter of relative and nonsensical opinion. The utopia they were hoping for is nothing but an illusion and a tool to exploit their consciences, so religious leaders can fulfill their egotistical agendas.

Further, most religions are merely projections of male-oriented obsession to control the world, a means to fantasize fulfilling patriarchal wishes to gain superhuman powers to cope with the challenges of daily life and dominate the world. Religion ascribed the power to dominate the world, but rather than to a frail common man, to someone who never fails—the patriarchal God. Each of the male-projectors had different specific concerns in life, and varied social and cultural settings where they lived, so the products are various Gods. When one expounds and organizes his projection, the result is a belief that followers eventually institutionalize as religion.

And to control people's consciences, religion uses three major beliefs—God, God's will, and heaven. God is the character that one wishes to be an illusory superman. God's will is the mandate that one wishes life to be. Then believers venerate a proxy patriarch, God, as the means to mystically fulfill one's wishes in life—God's will—that the projector of a belief couldn't have realized. So what we now have are Gods that are imaginary-beings and God's wills that are self-centered wishes. But for what purpose? To ensure one's destiny in the paradise of the hereafter.

Let's take, for instance, celebrity preachers proclaiming God's will. Does God speak to them? Or do they just figure out in their offices what to say to fulfill their agendas? Their agendas might include larger buildings, amassing more money, expanding programs, expressing their prejudices and notions, and preaching what they understood from their study of other literature. Or merely teaching what they think is the meaning of the sacred text they've read.

So everything religious is human. That's why I would say that religion is one of the greatest hoaxes of our civilization. Why? Because people blindly deify one's egotistical, mystical notions as *the* divine revelation. They assume the oracle's notion is God's unquestionable voice for human beings. They then worship the portrayal of one's super-man as God.

Could we not just realize how ridiculous it is? Let's awaken to the truth that for centuries we were blind to the subtle exploitations of our conscience by religion, that we dreaded rationally criticizing the Gods we created. Why? Because we are fearful that evil would befall us in the present and our souls would perish in hell in the hereafter. Of course, there are a growing number of enlightened former believers. But they are afraid to disclose their rational realizations because of foreseen social reprisal. And reprisal is even worse in Islam, where bloodthirsty religious leaders are obsessed about imposing their vengeance, cloaked as God's judgment.

That's why I believe that for our society to become more civilized, we should transcend the absurdity of religions. I just can't understand why our modern society still gives preferential treatment to religion. Freedom of religion does not mean granting religions special status to regulate other worldviews and freedom of expressions.

I won't refute the fact there are nuggets of insights from ancient religious literatures that we can reapply to our present life, but it's foolishness to institutionalize these nuggets of insights and use them to colonize society with a uniformed mystical notion. This is what Christianity in the past, and Islam even until the present, have been avidly doing for centuries with the inhuman slogan, "Believe or die."

At least Buddhism has taken a more humane approach to religion, with its emphasis on compassion, nonviolence, and contentment in life. Other dignified models are Taoism and Confucianism. Although they are not religions as usually tagged by the Western academe, they offer people something more sublime than other religions. Confucianism offers a practical and noble outlook on human relations based on individual and communal gracious reciprocation. And Taoism provides a deep eco-conscious worldview that promotes a harmonious cosmic life. These worldviews are also divine, yet they are not as institutionalized as other religions, and obviously they're not colonizers too.

But imagine, for instance, China institutionalizing Taoism as the state religion. China then becomes a Taoist Empire, and its mission is to convert the world to Taoism so it can transform the world into a paradise. Everyone will have to do Tai Chi every day and live in harmony with nature. And by the way, these are not bad propositions. But I bet Christians and Muslims would exclaim: "This is just ridiculous and tyrannical!" But is this not what they have been doing for centuries? They have been exploiting one of the countless products of ancient human reflections as a tool to subjugate the world. Did the humane God really mandate religiously-rooted inhuman acts of global magnitude? Or is it just the result of the ridiculous notions and tyrannical propensity of the delusional spokesmen of God?

"Hmm," Krister reacted.

Probably, if not for the institutionalized and invasion-obsessed Christianity and Islam, what we call religion today would have been a more human and spiritual way of life, instead of becoming institutions for the dogged propagation of religious imperialism.

And *seventh,* the absurd incompatibility of varied claims about God. If there is a God, to be consistent with all religious claims, he should be one and not many. Who then among the Gods of all religions is the true one? I bet all religions, including their thousands of subspecies, are ready to die affirming their self-centered notions. If God exists, he should have revealed himself without contradictions.

An all-knowing, all-powerful, all-present God wouldn't, and just couldn't, allow confusion in his beloved creatures. It would be irrational to enjoy seeing his crowning creation fighting to the death over a simple and easily resolvable issue: who among them is right about him. Seeing his cherished human beings brutally killing one another in a competition for exclusive rights to be his worshipers and go to heaven would be like enjoying a vicious gladiator game.

Haven't believers realized their madness in sacrificing their lives, money, families, and careers, just for universally incongruent notions of exclusive franchise of the mythological God and an illusory heaven? It's difficult for them to awaken to their senses when they grew up with deeply rooted traditions.

When I was a kid, I heard about faraway countries. But I presumed they were not as civilized as my country and their education and technology were crude. When somebody told me the opposite, I just couldn't believe it. How could it be, when I lived in the best country in the world? Now, as an educated grown-up, I've discovered to my amazement that many people in my country still think so; although many universities in what I then called faraway countries have higher ratings than ours.

Why? It's all because of a rooted preconceived notion of cultural superiority. Now, intensify this notion hundreds of times with fear, indoctrination, obsession over life in the future, social pressures and threats, generations of entrenched tradition, and so on. What you get is unwavering religious conviction. The conviction becomes unyielding; the belief is always affirmed as the only truth, and the soul becomes enslaved to religion. So a religious soul, however absurd his worldview and way of life is, has only one focus: the conviction of being one of the privileged few, among the billions of humans on Earth, who has exclusive rights to God and heaven.

If God is wise and loving, he should be inclusive, rather than exclusive. Believers ironically teach that all people have freedom of choice, but they offer only two choices, the right way that is theirs, and the wrong way that is others. So who has rights to God and heaven? Christians only? Muslims only? Hindus only? And who among the numerous Christians, and who among warring Muslims? If you just think it through, religion is nothing but plain absurdity!

"Wow! Sounds like you're crucifying Christ again," Krister said.

"O ... oh! Krister, let's not forget our intellectual civility," Elise reminded.

"Oh, sorry, I'm just overwhelmed by Leith's talk," Krister said. "But—"

Elise interrupted, sensing Krister was about to argue with Leith. "Okay guys, let's take a break. Leith, coffee or tea? Krister what about you?"

"Your treat?" Leith asked.

"Sure!" Elise replied.

"Let me think ... hmm," Leith said.

"Still not tired of thinking?" Krister asked with a bit of sarcasm.

"Okay, I think I want the Gold Coast Blend," said Leith with a smile.

"And what about you, my dear Krister?" Elise asked.

"Just the House Blend."

"Sure, sir." Then Elise gently pulled up JK's right earphone and sweetly whispered, "Anything for you my dear?" JK took off his iWear and replied. "Well, what about a creamy chocolate drink?"

"Hmm, where shall I get it?" Elise replied looking around. "Okay, there is it," she said, pointing at a fridge.

"How did you find your movie?" Elise asked JK.

"Just great! How was your chat, guys? Did you enjoy it?" asked JK.

"It's great!" Leith replied, beaming with relief from the intellectual pressures in his soul.

"Now, it's your dad's turn to tell us what he believes, but before that, let me get your treats," Elise said, gently caressing Krister's back to soothe him from the shocking conversation with Leith.

"You look like my dad's girlfriend," JK said.

"Me? Why?" Elise asked with a charming look.

"Because you're doing that to my dad's back," JK answered, motioning with his hands.

Everybody laughed. "You're such a wonderful boy, you know," Elise replied, and gently caressed JK's head.

"Okay, guys." Elise went to get their treats.

Krister tried his best to quickly organize his thinking. *Leith has got to know this, he just missed the point. I do hope he'll get it this time*, he thought. "God please help me," Krister whispered in prayer.

After experiencing an intellectual onslaught, he needed strength and zeal to talk about his faith. He was passionate about his faith, but the onslaught had caught him off guard, so he struggled to organize his faith as intellectually and persuasively a manner as Leith did. While waiting for Elise, he hoped she would take a bit more time, so he could adequately organize his thoughts. He remembered the classical arguments about the existence of God, but he supposed Leith would already know them. So he thought he'd speak from his experience—his life-changing experience.

"Nothing is more unquestionable than a personal experience. Who knows, my life-changing personal testimony might lead him to find God." Krister was enthusiastic. *And after all these years, this could be the time God has prepared for him. I can't wait for him to come back to God,* Krister thought excitingly. With missionary passion, he waited for Elise to come and start the conversation ...

*Is God, indeed, merely
a metaphor of our patriarchal wishes?*

What more sustainable anchor
in human life is there than faith?

Why I Believe in God

Part I

lise came back with an enchanting smile that instantly lifted Krister's spirit.

"May I help you?" Leith asked.

"Oh, no! I'm fine," Elise replied.

"Here's your Gold Coast Blend."

"Thanks Elise."

"And here's your House Blend."

"Thank you, Elise, thank you much," Krister said. Elise thought Krister was just thanking her for the coffee; she wasn't anticipating anything beyond that.

"Oh, you're welcome. I'm excited to hear what you'll have to say. As excited as I was with Leith," Elise said. "Now, I have my China Green Tip and here's your yummy chocolate drink, JK. Now we're all set to go. Let's get the ball rolling again."

"Okay, it's my turn to finish the movie. Dad, remember the song that we used to sing? The last time we sang it together was when we had a cruise and you woke me early in the morning to watch the sun rising. Then we sang it together, 'A sunbeam, a sunbeam, Jesus wants me to be a sunbeam ...,'" JK sang.

"Thank you, my boy, thank you." Krister hugged JK and kissed him on the head. JK instantaneously instilled in him the courage to soar like an eagle. Inspired, his mind opened clear, and with zeal, he shared the best exposition of his faith ever. But could this be his last too?

"Okay, my friends, now let me tell you why I ardently believe in God," Krister said with enthusiasm he felt as never before ...

First, the likelihood of our human existence is more viably explained by a belief in God than a belief in fate. Just imagine this. We're personal human beings with complex personalities and thinking. We have intricate lives and relations. Above all, we are living beings. How can we, after all, come from non-living matter?

Consider this. Would you believe me if I told you a stainless steel spoon gave birth to a human being? Or would a couple who wants kids believe me if I told them to just put dirt in a laboratory dish and wait a few years, then your baby will come out of it?

"But...," Leith interrupted.

"Leith, remember," Elise said.

"That's okay, just make it brief," Krister answered.

"But we're not talking here about a few years, we're talking millions of years of evolution."

Of course, Leith here might say that indeed a bacterium will come out from the dirt in the dish, then for millions of years that bacterium will evolve into a complex being until it becomes a human being. Okay, say there is a remote likelihood. But what about the likelihood of life coming out of the stainless steel fork? Can life come out of this—a nonliving thing?

He showed the spoon.

Say our existence started from atoms, all bouncing around, but could those atoms become human beings by just colliding with one another? It's like saying that after we drop an atomic bomb new human beings will appear. How can these atoms become the thoughts of our mind? How can these atoms figure out career, sadness, happiness, honesty, integrity, and love?

And not only in origin could we see the likelihood of human existence as more viably explained with the belief in God. But also our life itself, our everyday human life. Where are we going as a species? What's our future? What's the future of the planet we live on? Imagine having children and then abandoning them in a desert, telling them they'll survive because, after some years, they'll evolve into healthy and happy human beings.

Does it make sense to entrust our precious life to the hands of evolutionary fate? No! It's unthinkable for normal human beings to do that. Why? Because we live life with sensible models, with a sense of purpose, with insight into our origin and destiny. We come from our parents; our parents love and raise us, then as we grow we learn to live a purposeful life. Now, take personal relationships out of our everyday life: life becomes void and meaningless. Why? Because, as human beings we are created to relate to one another. And the noblest foundation of our relationship with one another is our relationship with our Creator-God.

Elise was somberly recalling her broken relationships.

To believe that we exist by chance, and that our destiny is in the hands of fate makes life purposeless. Without God we lack a sense of direction. Without the divine-human relationship providing us the model, our human relationship becomes empty. We'd be like zombies walking every day, living like machines waiting until our batteries die out. Our meaningful life then becomes nothing but mere mechanical operation.

But think about this. Every day we see purpose and meaning in our life, we naturally express love to one another, we face life with confidence, and in times of fear we have an anchor to cling onto. In times of frustration, we have the Creator-God to call on, like children coming to their fathers in times of need. Remember the feeling we had when, as a child, we'd cry for help, and then find comfort in our father's or mother's arms? It was just wonderful! And that's what we experience, believing in God.

Think how uplifting it is to have a loving and caring parent-child relationship. It's comforting to know that someone who bore us into this world is a living person who cares for us amid the challenges of our daily life. That's what God is to all of us—and that's what unbelief in God couldn't provide.

"Hmmm." Leith and Elise nodded.

Second, belief in God brings about hope and noble values in life, more than disbelief in God. Imagine a life without hope because nobody cares for you?

Elise was somber again, while Leith seemed moved. Krister's talk about relationships struck a divine chord in their hearts.

To whom shall we go to in times of tragedy? When we have tried all possible means but everything keeps crumbling? When even our best friends have left us. When we feel alone in this world with nobody to help us amid our hopelessness? When we're losing our loved ones? To whom shall we go for comfort and hope?

Elise felt like breaking into tears but held on.

What shall we do? Consider ourselves not fit to live life because we don't have the power and luck to survive? See the implications of life without God?

"Excuse me, I just have to go to the comfort room," Elise said, rushing out, holding back her tears. She looked around and nobody was in the washroom except her. She cried, recalling her heartaches from a series of broken relationships. Her beloved dad, to whom she had always leaned on for comfort, was gone. She felt so lonely and alone, especially when she needed him most, and he was no longer there.

After letting off steam, she washed her face and tried to smile to hide the misery she'd been carrying for years. Then she went back to the table.

"Sorry about that. Go on, Krister," Elise said.

Krister continued.

I know each of us has our difficulties in life. Now, if you will please, just try this before going to bed tonight. Think of your serious disappointments. Then pour it out to God. Just open yourself, talk to him like you would to a loving and caring father, and be frank—tell him everything, both the good and the bad.

Pour it all out. Then tell him your dreams in life, what you wish could have been different. If you feel like crying, cry. Anyway, nobody is there to listen to you except yourself and God. I bet I don't need to rationalize to you why you need to believe in God—you'll just experience its significance in your life.

You see, denying God is hard on the soul. Why? Because of the feeling that comes with rejection. When you reject God, you reject the anchor of human soul cherished throughout human civilization. Religion is soft on the soul, and is therapeutic too. From the singing of hymns, praying to let off steam, and sharing each other's testimonies of answered prayers, religion gives us comfort and eases our souls when we are troubled. These are benefits that denying God cannot provide.

Another is that there is no more sublime source of values than God. Yes, there are failings in religion, and I agree there are instances when human beings have created gods according to their images. But you see, faith in God enables us to cherish life in a more fulfilling way. In God we see the models of the ideals of human life and relationships. God teaches us that love, instead of lust or selfishness, should be the basis of our relationships.

But it wasn't lust, I did it all in love, Elise thought.

In fact, most religions teach us to be kind and compassionate to one another. The cruelties we see in history are not because of religion itself. Its root is outside religion, usually human injustice. Religion merely becomes a means for people to anchor their hopes while they're fighting for the injustices inflicted upon them.

Some people stereotype Islam as a terrorist religion. But there are also peace-loving Muslim countries who don't terrorize the world, nor conquer other countries. All they want to do is enjoy their God-given lives. And you don't see a Christian Empire now terrorizing and conquering other countries.

Of course, there are wars among countries with Muslims, Christians, and Hindus. But these wars are not religious in and of itself. The underlying issues are often the result of exploitations perpetrated by secular-minded people. These are not religious people, but secular people with political and materialistic agendas. In fact, at times they even use religion to hide their true secular identity and wishes.

However, with faith in God, we just don't think of human life as a cheap commodity that just emerged by chance. It's sacred and precious because God created it so. We see our fellow human beings not just as products of fate, but as dignified creatures of God. Why? Because it's God's will for them to exist and enjoy the beauty and wonders of life.

You see, our perspective of life changes. Instead of insecurity we have faith. Instead of fatalism we have purposeful living. Instead of pessimism we have optimism. Everything in this world looks bright when we see it as a God-cherished creation. Our outlook in life becomes verdant rather than withering. If we love life and want to enjoy life, there's no substitute for faith in God.

216

Third, God has been an essential and most cherished part of our civilization since it began. Taking him out would result in emptiness, both in our social and individual lives. It's like biological parenting, take it away and our human lives fall apart. Faith in God or, let me say, religion, is spiritual parenting. If we take it out, our human life falls apart too. Since the beginning of human civilization, we have always had spiritual inclinations. It's part of who we are as human beings. We are not just rational beings but also emotional, social, and spiritual. To take spirituality out of us, to debunk our faith in God, is making us less human.

Look, for example, at the importance of religion in the emergence of many societies. Many nations have historic roots of faith in God. Even China, the historical dynasties that ruled it had their deities. Russia, despite being the former center of the atheistic USSR, is the seat of Russian Orthodoxy. England, US, France, Germany, Italy, Denmark, as well as Latin American and Asian countries, all have religious roots. So did, of course, the great ancient civilizations like Egypt, Babylon, Greece, and others. Take religion out of these societies and they lose their rich heritages and historical identities. Instead of faith there would be a value-less culture without deep motivation for realizing the common good of the people.

Religion is not just about different ways of approaching God. In its deeper sense it's about us grasping at divine meaning in life amid our human limits. The answers we find, though different, have the same essential role: giving us a transcendent anchor to keep us going in life so we can find life worth living even amid difficulties. Religion enables us to overcome difficulties in life. It's one of our indispensable coping mechanisms. And we need it, both in our personal and social lives. Take this essential coping mechanism out, and we would significantly lessen our survival. Without it, our life becomes imbalanced and abnormal.

Let me cite practical circumstances here. What shall we do when someone passes away? Just bury the body without—at least—a service that brings about a sense of sacredness to life? Now, we are seeing many civil marriages nowadays, but mind you, most couples still regard church weddings as more meaningful than civil ceremonies. Look for example at the corporate world, where people are materialistic. People still believe that a religious ceremony inaugurating a new building can bring blessings. The absence of religious blessings, on the other hand, infuses an eerie ambiance. Even the materialistic world still leans on a transcendent power to ensure its success.

Throughout history, and in all societies, the sense of human need for God is always there. Suppressing or ignoring it is not only spiritually, but also psychologically and socially unhealthy. Life is not just about what's reasonable or logical, it's also about good feelings, fulfilling relationships, an awareness of our connectedness with the whole creation, a sense of awe and wonder, faith, hope, love, and so on. Life is a multidimensional unity. So we enjoy life and find it fulfilling when it's whole and wholesome.

The talk of enjoying a whole and wholesome life reminded Krister of how happy his life was when his family was still whole. Now, he enjoyed life with his son, but how he wished to have a whole and wholesome family again. The thoughts made him pause for a few moments, reflecting on his life.

"Hello, are you there?" Elise asked.

"Oh! Yes, sorry!" Krister replied.

"Something wrong?" Elise asked.

"No, not exactly, I just remember something. But anyway, where am I?" Krister asked.

"You're beside me, my dear," Elise joked.

Elise and Leith smiled.

"You're talking about your third reason that God is part of our civilization and denying him can lead to an imbalanced social life," Elise said.

"Oh, let me continue with my fourth point after sipping my House Blend coffee," replied Krister.

Why I Believe in God
Part II

*N*ow let me point out my *fourth* reason that I believe in God: worshiping and praying to God provides relief from the deep distresses of human life, and spiritually unites us with the unfailing God. We need God when we are facing giants in our life. Where else can we go to for help when we have reached our human limits but to the Infinite One?

We have to accept that part of being human is our limited capabilities. We are still creatures, though crowning works of God. At times, there are aspects of our life that we cannot control despite how ingenious we are. Despite how advanced our scientific knowledge, we still can't solve all the mysteries and problems of life. We need someone to lean on. We need someone to whom we can express our distresses in life or else we implode or explode.

Praying to God, communicating with the One who knows all about us, is the most uplifting and empowering means for us to cope with life. It refreshes our will to move on, reenergizes us both physically and mentally, and gives us a fresh outlook on life. Why? Because not only do we have to let off the steam of the pressures in life, but we are also uniting ourselves with our Creator and tapping into the divine creative power. We could feel as if the whole universe were with us, renewing our lives, and enabling us to transcend difficulties.

Millions and millions of people in the world can testify what this means, and what God has done in their lives. They can tell story after story about how God worked miracles in their lives amid seemingly hopeless circumstances: sickness, broken families, and marriages, shattered careers, bereavement, and other tragedies in life. Many of them are respected and educated people also, people who are not superstitious at all, but believe that human beings were created with divine purpose.

And not only the so-called good people in society, but even those we call undesirables have found new life in God. These are the people who could have continued living a life that endangered society, but when they found God their lives changed. I cannot scientifically explain this, but this experience is real when one believes in God. One of these

222

days, you may try it yourself, and see if it works. There's nothing to lose in trying, you know.

By the way, why do we, as human beings, have a natural inclination to cling to a power beyond us when facing insurmountable problems in life? Why don't we have the natural inclination to just figure it out? Every day it's our nature to figure out how to live, but in crisis situations it's also our nature to call on God for help.

Even those born in atheistic societies may not realize this, but indeed in crisis, they look up beyond Earth to grasp at something beyond human to help them. As creatures of God, we have the natural sense of spiritual linkage with him, although we express it in various ways. It tells us that by nature, we are worshipful and prayerful to the One who created us. It's the divine stamp in our nature, the stamp that remains in our being both here and in life after.

Fifth, in God we see a powerful motivation for achieving our personal and social ideals of life. Secular motivation alone is not enough to passionately empower us to become noble human beings. Politics and philosophy have tried, but couldn't come close to the impact of faith in God in realizing our human ideals.

Take for example the ideals of freedom in the US. Where did they come from? Faith in God! That's where the pioneers found inspiration. Yes, the pioneers were not perfect, but as they continued on their journey of faith, they also progressed in their efforts to realize the ideals of national life. Because of their faith in God, they established the democratic ideals of America. If not for this ideals, probably American today could be a country that suppresses human rights.

Look at the many humanitarian Christian organizations altruistically serving the world. How many millions of people, adults and children, men and women, have found hope in life amid privations, because of loving and caring Christians? The millions of dollars they spend on humanitarian efforts could have been spent on luxuries that meant nothing except to boost one's ego. But faithful believers spend it instead in noble causes to save lives. Why? Because of their faith in God. We can never solve all the problems in this world, but at least those who believe in God are touching and changing many lives around the world.

Every time we worship God, we see the ideals of love, compassion, freedom, equality, dignity of human life, orderly society, and a sense of togetherness in creating a paradise on Earth while waiting for the grand restoration of the paradise lost. Every time believers congregate, they celebrate life on Earth, thanking their Creator for its wonders and beauty, while also committing to making life on Earth a reflection of the heavenly.

Secular education alone is not enough to instill sublime human values and ideals of life. All it can do is promote theories about human life. Secular education produces students knowledgeable of various theories about human life but empty of the passion to make life more fulfilling for all.

Why? Because transforming human life and humanizing the society are not just about intellectual enrichment. It's about transforming the human soul. And only transformed people can become agents of transformation. One of the most sublime contributions of faith in God is transforming human life. A society that believes in God always asks, "Are our acts divine and humanizing?" A secular society can do anything without the divine reference that serves as the conscience of society. Look what happened to Cambodia in the communist Khmer Rouge regime. About 2 million Cambodians were killed by their own government through political execution, starvation, and forced labor. That's how inhuman a society can become when society takes away faith in God.

And show me a truly atheistic society that has both survived and progressed. The USSR fell down. China is not totally an atheistic society for it does recognize religion, realizing that it can't just wipe it out. Why? Because various religious beliefs are also embedded in its people and history. Faith in God is an essential part of the history of many nations. It's the root of their ideals as free and dignified countries. It defines who they are and where they are going. To strip away faith in God would be to strip many nations of their history and identity.

Further, faith in God boosts our efforts in promoting the ideals of human life. To speak about the ideals of human life in mere secular terms is just like delivering a lecture that enriches one's knowledge but lacks passion for its realization. You see faith in God brings about passions for both personal and social humanization.

Imagine, for example, during an emergency, somebody just softly says, "There's a fire and we need to leave the building." Do you think people will believe that message? Most probably not, because though the message is there, the expression lacks urgency. That's what happens when we promote human ideals without the power and expression of faith. With the conviction that God is behind us, our promotion of the ideals of our being human, such as deep recognition of the sacredness of human life, equality, justice, and benevolence—changes. It becomes life-changing.

And *sixth*, reality is not just human or merely about what we see and touch. It's larger than that. Often, people rationalize that creation, God, miracles, prayer, Bible stories, resurrection, and even the existence of Jesus, cannot be scientifically proven. But you see, our knowledge is so feeble that what we now figure out, we also debunk later with new discoveries. And what we presume as not existing before we later recognize as real. Before we think that only Earth is habitable. Now we're entertaining the idea that there can indeed be other habitable planets. In fact, now we have habitable space stations.

Who would have believed, in the Middle Ages, for example, that it's possible to talk to each other in a box that can send voices miles away? Who would believe that you can take a virtual painting of a person through what we now call photography? Or even watch the ancient theatrical plays via airwaves? Those were the realities that were beyond human grasp before. But now they're just common.

Before the onset of the industrial revolution, we thought of power as, literally, horse-power. Then we tapped dirty oil and our idea of power changed. Now we also know there are still other powers from nature that we could tap, sound and light waves, atomic and solar energies, etc. We even know now there is a physical healing power in positive thinking. And some scientists are even now talking about multiple dimensions of reality. We also know now that black holes exist, where time could possibly be eternal. And we are discovering other planets and galaxies that show reality is much larger than we thought. Our universe is ever expanding. And what we now call the edge of the universe is merely the farthest that can see using our latest technology. And our technology is always advancing. Science recognizes that we cannot limit reality to what we usually see and touch. Then why can't science also accept the likelihood of the existence of God?

Some people say that by simply looking closely at all the Gods religions are worshiping, we can assume that God is merely a human creation. Look at the stories they've invented, their conflicting characterizations of the nature and ways of God, they're nothing but products of human speculations. But what if there is, indeed, the Creator-God that transcends all religious portrayals? And what if religions see just the various aspects of one Supreme Being that are not, after all, contradicting? We have various religious views because people also have varied experiences in life. That variety of expression and views about God does not necessarily mean there is no God.

Just as, for example, after our summer break here in Niagara, we'll be expressing in various ways our experiences. Just because we have varied views and experiences about Niagara, doesn't mean Niagara does not exist at all.

Even here in Niagara, there are still countless nonphysical things that we can't all see and touch and are beyond our personal experiences and awareness. For example, there are a variety of emotions that individuals, families, and friends, experience coming here. Simply because we do not have the same experience as others, we can't assume that there's nothing real about Niagara. Saying so does not make sense. Those who don't believe in God would even entertain the idea there could be aliens with higher intelligence than us. Why can't they also entertain the idea of a supernatural being with the highest intelligence in the universe?

You see, though unbelievers may think of the creation of the universe by a personal God as myth, the likelihood of humans being intricately created by the Grand Designer is much greater than just emerging by chance. The likelihood of an outer space collision creating a laptop is ridiculous. Even more ridiculous is the likelihood of that collision creating the universe and human beings with more complex natures and functions than a laptop computer.

In fact, it's more mythical than the creation story. Would you believe that out of the big-bang a Rolex signature watch can come out? It's nonsense, right? But this is exactly what unbelievers in God are saying. And remember that living beings and life are more complicated to make than nonliving things. It's much easier to create a nonliving thing than a living being. The likelihood of the existence of a well-designed and complex living being through atomic collision is just absurd.

With the vastness of the universe, we just cannot confine reality to human reality. It's more scientific to say, as in Star Trek, to go where no human beings have dared to go before. Yes, I agree that Christians based their idea of heaven on the ancient belief that the world had three stories: heaven, Earth, and hell. But that was the worldview before. The essence of heaven is not about the world as having three tiers, it's about the place where the ideals of human life can become reality. It's the prototype of what human life should be.

Heaven, after all, is not just an illusory place. It's possible that somewhere in the universe there is a mega-planet whose topography, ecosystem, climate, and whole conditions are most suitable for perpetuating perfect human life. With our infinite universe, such a possibility is not remote. Einstein's scientific theory of time even speaks of the possibility of eternity. And look, for example, at the longevity many people today enjoy in First-World countries due to advancement in medical science and an improved way of life. Some countries even have minimal crime. The belief of God preparing heaven for human beings is not, after all, that superstitious, it's scientifically probable.

230

Simply because there are various interpretations of God that seem superstitious, we immediately debunk the existence of God. For example, medical science too had its superstitions in the past. Imagine the life-threatening notion that draining one's blood can cure all diseases. Imagine debunking the possibility of a cure for human diseases just because of the misconceptions in the past.

So why don't we advance our knowledge of God and his creation instead of dismissing it and leaving it in the hands of the superstitious? Imagine what medical science today would be today if we just left it to the 'medical expertise' of the past whose knowledge was in its infancy stage. Imagine what travel would be today if we had discarded the possibility of having airplanes because it was beyond ancient knowledge.

You see, the universe is full of endless possibilities, so could we not entertain the possibility of the existence of the highest of all beings we call God? Amid the vastness of our universe, could we not also entertain the possibility of another form of existence where eternity and perfection is real? Today, for example, we have voice-activated machines. Does this not at least imply the possibility that an omniscient Creator could indeed create our world through voice activation, as in the Biblical creation story?

If we want to think more rationally and scientifically, I think entertaining the idea that God exists is even more rational and scientific than denying it. Why? Because what's more rational is entertaining the idea that other possibilities exist and that traditional notions can be questioned. To be so dogmatic as to say that what we now think is unquestionable, is irrational. The progress of science depends on our motivation that we still have more to learn, more to explore, and more to discover. If we consider what we now know as final and unquestionable, then there's nothing more to learn. And we move back to a non-scientific outlook in life.

I'm not so naïve as to say there are no superstitions and myths in Christianity. I am also critical of people claiming to hear the voice of God mandating them to do something. I don't believe in healer-preachers claiming to have divine power to heal all sorts of diseases. If this is true, they should go to every hospital in the country and lay hands to all the sick. Lately, of course, we even heard the news of a marriage breakup of a famed healer. If God is with him, why can't he solve his marital problems? I also recognize there are many conscience-exploiters. They manipulate people to materially enrich themselves, and promote their delusional agendas.

However, there are also many other preachers who God has used to bring healing and transformation to the lives of millions of believers. And these are honest and sincere believers who live modest lives with moral integrity. In times of crisis, they have given us hope and inspiration to move on in life. They helped us get through tough times. Take, for example, Billy Graham. He impacted millions of lives throughout the world, including presidents and many other educated and respected people.

I know there are people who get frustrated with institutionalized religions like Christianity. I also have a long list of discouragements with Christianity. This includes:

- Racial segregation and prejudices
- Politicking and often-manipulative bureaucracies
- Bickering both inside the church and among Christian denominations
- Fundamentalism
- Dogmatism of theologians, as though they are already as omniscient as God
- Cultural imperialism, and other issues

And worse of all, I'm also aware of the tragic brutalities Christians and Muslims have done to others and to one another. But I know and believe that God transcends all these trivial and unfortunate matters that many institutionalized religions have brought. I also firmly believe God is just trans-sectarian and is the God of all. God, being God, is much larger than any religion can speculate. But simply because I experience frustration with religion, shall I deny his existence? No! In fact I want even more to explore my faith in God beyond the traditional portrayal of institutionalized religions like Christianity, Islam, and Hinduism. That's why I'm also exploring fresh meanings of my faith in God beyond traditional religion. Give it a try in your life too. Who knows, it might lead you to something life-changing and uplifting also.

"Well, Krister," said Elise, "I thought you were like most Christians I've met that were fundamentalist, narrow-minded, and judgmental. If Christians were as open-minded as you, probably many secular people would be more interested in giving religion a try. I did try it before, but I was so disgusted."

"Well, try it again and see how it works," Krister replied.

"Hmm, now you're beginning to convert us," Leith joked.

"Not convert in the sense of bringing you to a particular church so I could promise and assure you of salvation, not that stuff. Something more fulfilling and life-changing," Krister replied, expressing fresh passion.

"You mean something like what this audio book is saying?" Elise replied showing him her audio book.

"Well, I haven't heard that one yet. So why don't we make a deal? I'll get a copy of that audio book and listen to it. Then tonight, as I mentioned earlier, you guys spend time talking to God and pouring out your serious concerns in life to him. Do we have a deal?" Krister asked.

"Okay, we have a deal," Elise replied.

"Now, what do you want us to do then, Leith?" Elise asked.

Leith said, "Think of instances in your life when you tried reaching out to God and nothing happened. And think of the breaking news and events in the world, and see if God is there. Okay, so let's try each other's experiment in life, and see what happens to us afterward. Deal?"

"Here's to our journey of personal discovery," Elise said. They parted with a glass toss. Not expecting that they were tossing glass for the conversation that will unravel the anchor to the human soul they were seeking for quite a time.

"Now it's my turn, and you better listen to me guys. What I say could change the way you see life as a whole and not just how you see God," Elise said.

*What's the answer
to the restlessness of our souls?*

How can we ever be certain
of realities beyond us?

Why Nothing Is Certain

Part I

Elise continued.

Well guys, let me tell you that believing or denying the existence of God is the same. Why? Because they assume that our knowledge of reality is certain and final. We can never fathom reality. What we think of as reality is only what we immediately experience with our five senses. And we can't even experience all of our immediate reality. How can we then be certain of realities like God, heaven, and so on, that overwhelmingly transcend our immediate surroundings? And how can we also be certain of denying God?

Our knowledge, our worldview is ever changing. Is there certain and final knowledge even in scientifically verifiable studies? No! What we now recognize as standard information, we later dismiss as obsolete. We can see this recognition and debunking in medicine, engineering, space studies, and in many other scientific fields. That's why I'm an agnostic. Because all our experimentation and rationalization is just provisional, depending on our individual sensory experiences.

One reason I see agnosticism as the most sensible worldview is that our views of God and reality are merely contradictory theories. Despite 'scholarly developments,' our knowledge is nothing but mere products of our self-centered philosophizing. Why do you think we have varied ideas about God, psychology, philosophy, medicine, and e-ven the origin of the universe? Because different people think differently; different proponents promote different understanding. So what we have is a world flooded with all sorts of conflicting ideas that are nothing but various kinds of information and varied ways of looking at reality. They may be sensible to others, but not to everyone. No one can set a specific standard of knowledge for all. Even in our measurements, the world still can't agree on one standard. Some uses English units, others metric system.

And belief in God is the leading example of all these ambiguities. Why do we have varying beliefs about God? It's simply because different proponents see God different-ly. Further complicating the original proponents' teachings are the various ways their followers interpret their beliefs. The result is the buildup of generations of conflicting ideas with many beliefs and sub-belief groups. Religion has done nothing more than spread more confusion to our already confused world.

What I just couldn't understand is why, even though our modern civilization is considered educated, we still have people dumb enough to die for a particular view of God. What they're dying for is nothing but a mere theory about God. I'm not just talking here about fundamentalist Muslims but fundamentalists in all religions, including Christianity. How many Christians have suffered and died believing that their notion of God will assure them of the heavenly paradise in the hereafter?

One of the most life-degrading effects of religious beliefs is martyrdom, found among Muslims, Christians, Shinto in World War II, Sheiks, and others. Those martyrs just couldn't open up their minds and see the larger reality of life. The years of dogged indoctrination since their childhood days, led them to assume that they alone, among the billions of people in the world, hold the secret of life in the hereafter.

Religion is one of the most deceitful human creations that plagues our society. And it's ridiculous that our civilized society still treats religions in special ways, like giving them tax breaks and protecting them from criticism. Can't we just see how religion has been exploiting, as Leith said, not only people's consciences, but also their money? Look at the grand buildings of many churches, mosques, and temples. If religion is that altruistic, they should have modest places of worship that are more natural as the place of worship of the creator of nature. They could have instead spent their money relieving human sufferings.

Listen to the speeches of clergies. Either they're mimicking motivational talks christened in religious terms, or delivering messages according to their personal agendas. Did God speak these messages to them, or have they prepared these in their offices using books other authors wrote? And believers just say 'amen' as if God has spoken to them. Couldn't believers awake from their deep slumber of ignorance and insensibility?

It's the same in the academe. We have many religious scholars, even coming from globally-respected universities, claiming that their interpretation of God is the most truthful of all, and they all disagree. I can't understand why reputable universities still have theology departments. I think religion could be more sensible if we changed it to lifestyle studies rather than as theological or religious studies. In this sense, people could deduce and find meanings about choices to various lifestyles, rather than focus on who has the only rights to heaven.

Number *two* point that I'd like to bring about is that universal reality is much larger than our tiny human reality. How can a tiny human being grasp all that is overwhelmingly beyond it?

I'm amused at Leith's illustration of the ant. If we think of the Earth as a speck of dust in this vast universe, our knowledge is nothing but a speck of the universal information too. Imagine, for example, when one claims to proclaim the will of the infinite God. You mean that out of billions of people in our world, only that person knows it? That amid the unimaginably countless planets in the countless planetary systems of the countless solar systems in the countless galaxies, only that person knows the mystery of God? That's ridiculous!

And the most ridiculous teachings in religions that I see involve God's will. Why? Because, my dear Krister, while claiming God as infinite, it also confines God to the tiny notions of prophets, clergies, and theologians. Nonsense! When can believers ever awaken to the foolishness of religions? I know that even when they realize the folly of religion, it's still hard for them to reject God. Because they're afraid that if they deny God, a curse may fall upon them. Or that their family and friends, and society in general, will reject them too. They're afraid of becoming social outcasts.

Look, for example, at the idea of life in the hereafter. Many Christians, claiming to promote the love of Christ and asserting that God is a loving God, also love to cherish the idea that someday sinners will suffer extreme pain throughout eternity. That's one of the most sadistic and ironic beliefs I've ever heard! When we study human history and the dynamics of our civilization, we discover something mundane about religion. It's merely a potpourri of believers' wishes amid their hardships in life and their limited power to control the forces of nature. And, as in the case of belief in hell, their wishes to punish others they don't like but must tolerate in the present.

The ideas of God and heaven are just projections of human wishes for rewards, and punishments that believers can't realize in their present lives. These are all symbols of both personal and communal longings. That's why religion is a myth, the symbolic representation of humanity's yearnings in life. Because believers cannot realize these yearnings in the present, they fantasize about it. And to make it more personal, they project the ideal person to realize it. Thus they have the figure of the all-knowing, all-powerful, and

243

ever-present God to ensure their myths and fantasies—at least in the hereafter, if not in the present.

Then they make this relative and ambiguous symbolization the basis of the way they see universal reality. They cherish this symbolization because it gives them an anchor for their fantasies, both in the present and in the hereafter. They treasure this notion so much they don't want anybody to take it away from them, so they are willing to become martyrs so they don't lose them. Yet it's nothing but a delusion; to use Dawkins' term, "God Delusion."

But is religion all bad? No! I also see good ideas and practices in religion. What makes it bad is when people begin institutionalizing religion and making it an exclusive enclave and licensee of heaven. But considering that, although our reflections are relative, they are also the products of human creativity. And they can also contribute, as bits and pieces, in forming our grand, although relative, mosaic of fulfilling human life.

That's why, as I just mentioned, we need to transform religion into a lifestyle study, and consider the varied lifestyle contributions not as competing but as contributing to a grand synthesis of human life. It's only then that out of the products of human culture we could see something divinely uplifting for our personal and social life. But again, we should not impose religion as the only answer to human needs. We also need to recognize that not only religion, but also other aspects of our culture contribute to the grandeur of human life. These include art, music, literature, social relations, health and fitness, general education, sports, films, and so on.

But look at what believers have done to the overall human life. They truncate the rest and impose religion as the basis of all aspects of human life. This imposition does not only dehumanize our soul and spirit, but also disconnects us from one another, and makes fragments out of our whole and wholesome life. We need to trash the fanaticism and exploitation of the tiny few who claim to hold the secret of the vast universe and impose their delusional notions as the only answer to fulfilling human life.

"Wake-up my dear, Krister! Just see the reality!" Elise said, gently tapping Krister's shoulder.

Three, there's nothing absolute about our knowledge of human life and the world. Science changes, our way of life transforms, and our ideas of morality adapt to new situations as we progress in our civilization. Even religious beliefs and practices take on new forms when society's way of life changes due to technology.

If our knowledge of human reality is not absolute, how certain are we of our knowledge about the reality beyond our world? Even in mathematics, two elements are not always two. It could be two or one, depending on the sign that our civilization has figured out. Are there also other dimensions of life where two elements could be thousands or whatnot? I don't know. But is it possible that there are other dimensions of life in the universe where mathematics is different from ours? There could be.

Before, we thought only God could create life. But now with advancements in biological sciences and genetic engineering, we can indeed recreate life. We can even create sea monkeys. Before we thought reality was just one-dimensional; now we have virtual reality. Fifty years ago we regarded our sciences and technologies as advanced. Now, those sciences are obsolete. There are even a number of respected theoretical physicists now who are propagating the possibility of the existing of the multiverse that can radically transform our concept of reality.

Mind you, if Leith could go back to Jesus' time and show the apostles modern gadgets, like a film projector or even just a microphone, they might be split as to whom to choose as messiah. People would look at the projected film as the grandest of the heavenly visions. Because while divine vision is usually private, everybody would be able to see it. You could imagine everybody worshiping Leith as the anointed of God. More so, he could project his voice using the microphone. People then would revere him as the voice of God speaking from the heavens. Let him fly a combat helicopter—if you know how to, Leith—and even the mighty Roman Empire would fall on their knees worshiping you as a god with superhuman power.

Our creativity enables us to discover and make inventions, shapes fresh worldviews, and brings us to various stopovers in our history. But our journey never ends. Our life and perspective of life is never stationary. Each stage in our history brings freshness to the human way of life. We are not routinely functioning machines, but beings full of life. When we confine our life with a particular myth, we are not only suppressing our creativity, but also dehumanizing our civilization. We become submissive to myths rather than creative and bold.

Leith mentioned the brutalities of religions. Indeed, religions have brought more dehumanization than humanization in our society, both past and present. History tells of many instances when religious people senselessly punished intellectuals because they did not accept as truth the will of God as speculated by so-called 'spokesmen' of God.

The amusing irony though, even to this day, is that while many religiously-rooted universities would like to appear as advanced academe, they still cling to their mythical traditions. Why? They embrace science but impose only the science that promotes their religious beliefs. They still consider religious myth the basis of modern learning. It's like saying, "Okay, you can do space explorations, but only what reveals how flat the Earth is." "Why?" an open-minded professor may ask. And the rectors respond, "Because it's the truth from God that our clergies have known since they were babies. And if you don't believe it, we shall expel you." Sorry for my sarcasm, but that's exactly what many supposedly reputable centers of learning are still today. You can study science, philosophy, and other disciplines, but only that which confirms the veracity of their religious myths.

And why do we see those nonsense fanaticism resulting in horrible acts? Simply because many lunatics think that what their anointed 'prophet' says is the real voice of God, not sensibly realizing it's just the voice of another lunatic like them. Lunacy begets lunacy. Now, tell me of any God-believing religion that has not done any inhuman and lunatic acts in history?

The guys laughed both at what Elise said and the way she said it.

"But if ever Christians engaged in war in the past, it's because they just wanted to defend themselves against marauders," Krister said.

I don't think so. History tells us that, in the past, Christians, Muslims, Shinto, and other religiously-rooted people did try to convert the world by the sword. The truth is, God-believing religions are imperialistic. Even though nobody attacks them, they still subjugate others, believing that their God commands them to do so—to convert the whole world into their religious empire. Have you watched the movie *September Dawn*? It's horrible! Just horrible! But mind you, this is just a tiny piece of the overwhelming horrors and cruelties religions have brought to our civilizations.

Because of our obsession to be certain with the hereafter, we created many ridiculous myths. And these myths degrade human life, oppress human freedom, and threaten the sanctity of human creativity. Human life, you know, is more sensible when we see it as progressive rather than static. This makes us grow. Growth and change is part of our nature, part of our being. When we continue to freely explore and progress in life without the constraints of religious myths, life becomes fulfilling.

By the way, I don't hate ancient sacred writings, for I also see treasured gems of wisdom in them. What I'm reacting to is the fanaticism toward institutionalized myths. I also wanted to explore ancient wisdom. That's why I'm excited to listen to Wayne Dyer teaching me about the wisdom of Lao Tzu. I'd like to learn the ideals of human life from ancient sages so I could relate these to my daily life. My sages include Lao Tzu, Moses, Jesus, Mohammed, Buddha, Confucius, and others. I like to sift the positive universal values from the destructive ones, so I can create a fresh harmonious worldview that is useful in my life without worshiping it as an idol. In this sense, I avoid the usual vanities that religion has brought.

I also see some uplifting values in religion. One of these is common among religions: compassion. In Christianity we find the model of a trans-ethnic compassion, as in the story of the Good Samaritan. In Islam it's compassion in the sense of denying one's self to set aside alms for the poor. Another is freedom. Judaism, for example, celebrates the Year of Jubilee, and it's also the time for freeing slaves from their masters. About human relationships, Confucianism teaches mutual respect and responsibility. Taoism teaches harmony with nature. Hinduism promotes transcendence from the stresses of materialistic world. Buddhism promotes compassion, nonviolence, and peace.

I'm not against the noble teachings found in religions for, as I said earlier, they are all part of our sublime civilization. What I despise is the lunacy of spreading and heeding the claims of divine will that fanatics use, time and again, to control people's conscience and even horrify our urbane society.

"Now, let me take a sip of my China Green Tip to cool me," Elise said.

The guys smiled.

"Ohh … wonderful! It's just so soothing to feel the tea calming my stressed mind and rejuvenating my weary body … hmm …" She sighed, gently closing her eyes, letting off the steam that pressured in her soul.

Why Nothing Is Certain

Part II

"Okay, now I'm ready," Elise said, smiling.

Four, if God exists and is omniscient, he should have given us a systematic and unified account of his being, will, and the secrets to finding fulfillment in human life.

Where is he amid all the confusions of beliefs about him? Where was he, for goodness' sake, when I was struggling in life? Leith mentioned communication. No sensible CEO, more so an omniscient Founder-Chairman of the universe, could just leave his beloved creatures squabbling to death over who among them holds the only truth about him—or if they all hold bits and pieces of truth about him.

Now, let me present to you a more sensible perspective of what religion calls divine revelations. Let's consider, for example, the Torah, the Bible, and the Koran. When we see similar ideas among them, it's not because God had revealed himself to the three chosen prophets. They are similar because the later writings carried over the modified ideas of the earlier writings. So we have a Christianity that is a Judeo-Christian religion. We have Islam that is an innovation of Judaism and Christianity in the backdrop of early Arabian social context. And we have Judaism that was also influenced by Ancient Near Eastern cultures. So the Old Testament myths, like the stories of creation and the flood, are similar to Mesopotamian myths.

When we study various myths in different cultures and history, we also see a common connection among them. But the connection is not about a unified and directly revealed account of God's creation or will. It's about the common symbols of human longings, mystical attempts to explain the unexplainable, and projections of human ideals.

You see there's a difference between writing an exposition and a letter. Any literate person reading texts knows the difference between one's expositions of his or her ideas, and a personal letter written specially for a loved one. If you read all the sacred writings, they're nothing but ancient expositions of myths. Of course, in the New Testament we also find letters, but God did not write those letters to his worshipers, human writers wrote them for others.

If God is as religious people believe him to be: a caring male founder, and CEO of the universe, he should have written us a concise and clear biography about himself. He should have written it on a special material that would last for centuries. And in a language that everybody throughout history could understand. Further, the letters should, at least, be in a grand and awesome form, to reflect his grandeur and that of the universe he founded. No CEO of a respected multinational corporation would leave it to third parties to speculate about what he likes to do in his firm.

Why has God not, personally and directly, left us a clear and unified account of the creation of the universe and what happened afterward? Believers just ignore the fact that Biblical stories were not direct revelations from God. In fact, the creation story did not originate from Moses. It came from civilization generations before Moses. Christians, of course, will be quick to say that he did—it's the Bible. But it was a myth retold from one generation to another, thousands of years before Moses and Jesus. Christians also ignore the fact that there were many variations of biblical manuscripts, aside from many other similar ancient literatures.

Imagine, for instance, a CEO telling employees that once upon a time, I voice-activated the existence of our company, and bingo, it appeared perfectly formed! But you guys messed up my company. And despite my having the supernatural power to command things into existence, I just won't do it. Why? Because I have given you the choice to enjoy life in the company or not. For those of you who messed up, eventually I will punish you for giving me many headaches. I'll wait till the company crumbles to do so. For those who like to live in the company, I authorize you to destroy those who don't, so I can recreate the company anew.

Good management? Of course not! This management style is as nonsensical as the story itself. Why? Because if God is a wise CEO and has the power to command the existence of his company, it's more efficient to spend a few seconds recreating it perfectly that allowing the mess to create further hardships for lifetimes. Or why not create a perfect company in the first place, so it won't endanger his employees?

Ah! What about the freedom of choice? Is it freedom of choice to let the good ones suffer the miseries the bad ones have caused? That's not about freedom of choice; in fact, it's injustice. Why not create two worlds: one for the good, the other for the bad? Then just let everyone choose which world they'd like to live in. In this scenario, there would be no victims among the good, only among the bad because they choose to victimize one another anyway.

And who are the bad anyway? Are they not misdirected human beings? If God existed, he could have ensured that everybody born is living in desirable ideal life conditions so they won't suffer defects and commit wrongs. Everyone could live harmoniously in a healthy and wholesome human society. But the reality is, there is no utopia, no human being can realize it, although we wish for it. So believers create their fantasy-paradise that only their imaginary super being, "God," can realize.

Because they have different personalities and situations in life, they also have different wishes about God and paradise. In their fanaticism, they become zealous in imposing their notions on others. They transform their belief in God to an imperialistic preoccupation. Blend this preoccupation with social and political causes, manipulation of conscience, money, and arms, and the world sees militant fanatics believing it is God's will for them to be horrifying and inhuman. Ridiculous and stupid!

So now, amid all the millions of deaths, including innocent children and infants, pregnant women, and feeble seniors—because of religiously-rooted wars since our civilization began—where is God? Nowhere, of course, because there is no God. If ever there are extraterrestrial beings more intelligent than us, they could also be busy coping with their challenges in life, if not just enjoying life. It's up to us human beings to figure out how we can, together as one human family, recreate a more harmonious and sensible life.

Human life is not about God, it's about us. When we become more human-centered—passionately exploring a more equitable, interconnected, and constructive life—our world will be a better place in which to live. We would become truly divine. So for me godliness is not about dogmas, churches, sects, theology, or other institutional religious matters, it's about giving birth to a deep sense of sacredness and dignity to the life we all live every day.

When we value human life and live by that valuing, we see beautiful and lovely human life blossoming, we complement and enrich one another as we give birth to our delightful garden of life out of our stale global society. This is more divine for me. And more realistic than expecting heaven to come from nowhere and in the hereafter, when we probably couldn't enjoy it anymore. True godliness is about making life on Earth more divine and dignified.

"So, Krister, I hope you don't think of people like me and Leith as devil's advocates. We too yearn for a fulfilling human life. Krister, are you here ...?" Elise asked while gently caressing Krister's back, thinking him dumbfounded.

Krister, however, was actually staring at Elise with a sympathizing and loving look.

"We're all here, Elise," Leith replied with a smile.

"Thanks, Leith. Now let me say my last point."

The *last* point that I'd like to say is: there is no essential difference between the life of believers and the life of non-believers. Except, of course, for an illusory expectation of having a preferred reservation in paradise.

How do we distinguish the life of believers from unbelievers? When others don't go to church and don't believe in God, does that mean they are murderers, criminals, child abusers, or whatnot? In fact, the same social problems exist among unbelievers and believers alike. Are there molesters among believers? Of course! We can't let the back-drop of clergy reverence make it easy to ignore the issues of molestation in the church. Sin committed inside the church is even more deceptive than sin committed outside the church.

What about fraud? How many churches milk their members while their organizations and clergies squander money on luxuries amid believers fantasizing rewards in heaven? Look at the assets of many churches. They're amount to more than a number of greedy multinational corporations who provide livelihoods to people. Look at the fraudulent belief that giving one tenth of your income to the church will earn divine approval. Imagine paying taxes to a heavenly kingdom? If God is all-sufficient, why does he need people's money?

Let's be candid here. Who needs the money, God or the religious institutions? Can God survive without our money? Of course, yes. Can religious organizations survive without our money? Of course not! Religious organizations simply cannot survive without the financial support of its members. They have utility bills to pay, staff salaries, building mortgages, and other operating expenses. But why teach that giving tithes is heavenly when the purpose is mundane? So the church could save more people? Oh, C'mon!

The idea of 'holy money' is nothing but a financial tool in spreading one's relative notion about God and life in the hereafter. Of course each church needs financial support. But why impose it by manipulating conscience? I don't know why governments are so ludicrous as to provide tax incentives for promoting theories of God. Religion is nothing but a philosophical business baptized with fear of an a-venging God.

If churches solicit donations because they want to serve the deprived and rejected human beings in our society, then it's a noble cause. And I do believe they do deserve tax breaks and even government support for humanitarian reasons. But for the state to give churches privileges so they can continue spreading their notions of God, and convert more people, is just a plain old scam, one that even our civilized and educated societies allow in the hallowed name of religious freedom. This is foolish. It means freedom for religious organizations to deceive people about their various and conflicting delusions of God and paradise.

Now let's take another issue to see if there is indeed a difference between the life of believers and unbelievers. The issue that's close to my heart, my dear friends: divorce. Are believers free from them? The rate of divorce among believers is as common as those among non-believers.

Elise made a charming yet sarcastic pause, expressing disgust about the divorce she'd been through. The guys smiled.

What about extramarital affairs? Don't tell me "holy" men and "holy" women are free from it. In fact, some religions allow multiple marriages. It's nothing but lust institutionalized. And why allow only men to have multiple wives, why not also allow women to have multiple husbands? The truth is, religious people are more chauvin-istic than secular. Look at how they treat women. Aren't women regarded as less divine in religion?

I think secular people even have more sensible ethics than the religious ones. Many secular people are family-loving and just want to live honest and decent lives. They do that because they love life. On the contrary, most religious people are trying to live good lives because of fear of punishment from a judgmental God. Imagine being punished by an eternal and horrifying hell. They're scared to death, so they have no choice but to be good.

Further, when secular people become generous and charitable, they do so because they like to. When religious people do it, they do so calculating their rewards in heaven. It's a selfish giving, rather than an altruistic one. So it doesn't matter whether one is a believer or not, what matters is the life one leads. And no religion can assure people that it can transform them from something bad to something good. In fact, at times religion makes people worse.

Of course, there are instances when criminals become believers through preaching, even when still in jail. But remember, these are people with imprisoned souls. As human beings, they want to get out of their miseries. It's not religion itself or the power of God that changes one's life, it is people consciously or subconsciously wanting to change.

It just happened that religious preaching was there as a tool for changing their life.

Transformation of life is not even exclusive in one's religion or church. Change happens to people in many other places and avenues. And not necessarily brought about by God mediating through a church or a preacher. For example, what about the lives changed through counseling sessions with secular counselors? Is God there too? If it is, then there's no need to confine him in a church. Some friends who converse and share their problems in a bar also experience transformation of life. And that's an irreligious place to experience a conversion of the human soul.

What about love and hatred? My goodness! I found no place more ironic than church, where the claim of love is coupled with hatred. In religion we see the love of God often deeply entwined with hatred of others belonging to different religions or sects. In fact, because of the love of God, religious people would destroy others. Why? Because religion is the most self-centered and exclusivist of all our social institutions.

It's self-centered because sectarian beliefs become the center of human life. And people who don't live the prescribed life are regarded as outcasts who should be converted either by choice or force. It's exclusivist because it regards itself as the only way to God. Other ways are regarded as heretical and devilish. This blindness in religion is so grave that when believers do devilish and horrible acts in the name of their faith, they ludicrously think it's divine. So we could even see more murderers among religious fanatics than resolute atheists or agnostics.

The only superficial difference I see between believers and unbelievers is the delusion of paradise in the hereafter. While many secular people live one day at a time, believers see every day as moving toward an end. And the end that they look forward to is the destruction of the world and their exclusive salvation. What a pessimistic outlook on life, what an egotistical delusion.

So I hope we are all sincere in listening to one another and setting aside our prejudices. After all, we belong to one human family, and are all as human as one another, regardless of our perspectives in life. And as a family, think how beautiful life would be if we joined our pieces together in the portrayal of a fulfilling grand mosaic of our human life and civilization. Instead of fragmenting it, why not make it whole? We all have our prejudices based on our experiences and sensory perceptions. But, together as one human family, when we transcend our prejudices and become open to the all-encompassing blend, we can create a more pleasant and harmonious life.

Leith said, "Wow, I'm astounded at what you said. It seems you're speaking outright from the heart, like me and Krister. And it looks as if we are all moving toward a new synthesis in our individual lives. I wonder: what will be the impact of our coffee talk on each of us?"

His remarks stirred up one another's defining moment. Their search for meanings amid their struggles in life took a fresh direction. While at the outset they were prejudiced on one another's outlook in life, now they understand that they all share a common journey in search of a sensible anchor to their soul that will guide them through life.

"So guys," said Elise. "We have heard each other. What next?"

"Are you guys staying for a few more days?" Krister asked.

"I'll be!" Elise answered.

"So am I," Leith said.

"Well what about another coffee tomorrow?" Elise quickly said. "It will be my treat again. But this time, instead of just saying what we think, why don't we ask and clarify each other's viewpoint, so at least we can have a clearer picture of how to blend our perspectives on life?"

"That sounds good," Leith replied.

"But no argument, just clarification. No debate, just a friendly conversation. And most of all, the willingness to sincerely listen to one another," Elise added.

"Sure!" Leith said.

"That will be great!" Krister said.

"Is JK still watching his movie?" Elise asked. "Looks like he's asleep, either bored with the movie or tired of waiting for us."

The guys laughed.

"JK, time to go." Krister gently tapped JK's shoulder, slowly waking him.

"Oh, how was it, Dad?" JK asked.

"Fine!"

"How about your movie?"

"Well, Dad, it's my third time watching it and every time I see it I discover more fun. It's so funny when God suddenly appears, and then suddenly disappears after telling Evan what to do. So guys don't be afraid when God suddenly appears, telling you how to become a superhero!" JK said with enthusiasm.

The guys smiled, thinking through the JK's words.

"And another one, don't be afraid when something strange happens, because that can be good too," JK added. "And don't forget to help one another. Don't leave someone without helping. And remember ARK means 'Acts of Random Kindness.'"

The guys smiled again, amazed at how a child's simple words could awaken their awareness to life's precious lessons.

"You're teaching us many lessons, JK," Elise said gently, caressing JK's head.

"Thanks," he responded.

"I'll see you around." No Elise said.

"Now we can go look around. C'mon Dad, I'm excited." JK stood and grabbed his dad's hands.

"See you guys tomorrow," Elise said.

"And thank you, Elise, for the coffee," said Krister while leaving and waving his left hand.

"My pleasure," Elise lipsynched.

"Thanks, Elise," Leith said, hugging her.

"My pleasure, Leith, my pleasure." Elise hugged him too with the warmth of her heart. "I hope we have opened Krister's mind," Elise said.

"I hope so too," Leith replied. "See you then." Elise waved at him with a sweet and charming look.

Hmm, interesting guys, the journalist thought. *They all speak with the same passion. But what will happen to each of them? That'll be interesting to see …*

266

The grandeur of the mosaic of life unfolds
when we bring together our answers
to the enigma of our existence.

ℰoul-Searching

ℰLISE went to Fallsview Casino to further steam off the restlessness in her soul. At least she'd vented her viewpoints earlier. But the restlessness of her soul still haunted her. After a couple of hours at the casino, she went back to her hotel room. Lying on the bed and staring at the ceiling she reflected ...

What am I really seeking for? I don't know ... I know Leith and I wanted to change Krister's notion of religion, but he has some points too. I still don't believe in God. The likelihood of the existence of aliens with higher intelligence is much greater than the likelihood of the existence of the God of religion. There could be beings in other planetary systems with more capabilities than humans. But even if they exist, I doubt they understand human life.

What about angels? My, my! That's a common myth Christians borrowed from another culture they call 'pagans.' Religion is nothing but a myth, expressions of the symbols of wishful reality. But where shall I go to find the answer to something I can't understand? I don't like religion. I don't like believing in God. I despise the certainty of knowledge.

But it seems what I'm looking for is something that ... I don't know ...

Don't tell me, Krister, you're beginning to convert me. No way! I'm still sensible enough, despite my frustrations in life. But could I, indeed, be seeking something mystical in life? Something beyond what's rationally sensible? Well, it's not a bad try. After all, there are many facets of human life. Just as I'm not certain of knowledge, I should not also be certain about denying the existence of other realities.

Gosh! Don't do that Elise ...

But should I not also be certain about denying the existence of God? Oh! No! I'm confused ...

Okay, say there is a highest being in the universe. But I don't think I'm that foolish to accept the Gods of religions. Besides, who among them shall I choose? There are just too many of them, so many forms, and nothing but speculation.

What's the answer I'm really seeking in life? And why am I seeking the answer when there's nothing certain in this world anyway? Yes, as far as information and knowledge, there's nothing certain, but I need to find something sensible in my life. I need something that, at least, gives me rest from my restlessness.

Or probably I'm just restless because of my frustrations in trying to find a lasting and happy relationship. Imagine no more intimacy, no more sweet kisses and exciting romances, no more arms to hold me, making me feel secure, no one close to talk to and share sweet nothings with at bedtime.

Am I just looking for a new relationship or something beyond that? Oh no! Elise don't lose your mind, don't you ever lose your mind. A mystical relationship with an imaginary being just isn't the answer. I couldn't deal with that; that's not a real person, that's a fantasy.

What I'm looking for is a real person, a real touchable relationship ... but I have already tried several times and all they gave me were heartaches.

"Ah! Hmm ..." Elise sighed then smiled.

What about flirting with either Leith or Krister, or both, and see who falls in love with me?

270

What if it's Krister? My goodness! He'll be preaching to me all day and all night. I couldn't imagine myself attending church services and singing those funny hymns, or having a "holy disco." That's funny, the church trying to draw disco-loving people to God? They're full of gimmicks nowadays to convert irrational people. Besides, how can I take care of a child? That's too much for me. Cooking food, waking up early in the morning, getting his child ready for school, attending school meetings, and so on. These are stress-inducers for me. I can't live like that.

But Krister looks like an honest and sincere man, different from all my exes. He's just a simple man, and being a single dad, that takes much patience, sincerity, and self-sacrificing love. Oh how I wish I could find a man like that. But why look for somebody else when he's already here? I could spark something beautiful. Besides, the way he looks at me tells me that he likes me. He's sort of having a secret 'love at first sight' thing with me. What if we have dinner together say in the Skylon Tower? That's the perfect place to spark a romance amid the awesome ambiance of the grand Falls …

Now what about Leith? Gosh! Both of us have compatible worldviews, but he'll give me more restlessness in my soul with his disbelief in anything beyond the material. Besides, he seems as carefree as I am. And yes, I'm carefree most of the time, but I'm also searching for something fulfilling and stable in life.

However, Leith is a suave professional guy, formal yet charming and classier than Krister. He's the guy who can go with me to parties. You know, the guy who looks good in a tuxedo or in casual wear. He'd be somebody I could be proud of to introduce as my dear husband.

But he also seems restless and mad about something I can't understand. As if he has an unresolved anger over something, probably God or whatnot. Like me, he's mad at religion. And although we're one in trying to change Krister's mind, we're still strangers to each other. We don't know each other's secrets. He doesn't know why I became an agnostic, and I also don't know why he became an a-theist. It looks like both of us have hidden secrets behind our masks.

Gosh! What shall I do? Let me try my audio book. And well, I promised Krister to try what he suggested before going to bed tonight. Just so I can tell him honestly tomorrow that I did it. No harm in trying it anyway. Okay, now let me listen to this guy and see if something good can come out of it ...

Krister and JK went for a ride on the *Maid of the Mist.* They were both awed by the grandeur of the Falls. JK kept on clinging to his dad's hands, scared of the enormous pressure of the falling water. JK stared at the Falls and the mist that rose from it. Krister though, on seeing families enjoying the adventure and fun together, became a bit sulky and began reflecting ...

How I wish my family were still together. I can imagine the fun we could have here. Yes, I'm happy that JK is with me, but how much happier I would be if my family were complete?

And where were you God, when I needed you most? Where were you when I lost my calling, and my wife left me for another man who was already married? You see, if you really cared for your children, you should have answered my prayers.

At times I would assume that what happened in my life was your will. Often, even after many prayers, undesirable events still happen in my life. And I just rationalize that it's your will anyway and something good could still come out of it. I believe you exist, but do you really answer prayers? Do you really work miracles in our lives today as you did in the past?

Forgive me for my doubts, but honestly there are times when I think that after you created us, you just left everything in our hands. Have you left us in the hands of fate? Have you abandoned us? Forgive me again, but many times

I pray because I'm afraid that if I don't a curse will fall on me. My prayers are now becoming mechanical, like letting off the steam of my fears and anxieties in life instead of that intimate conversation with you. Because you don't seem to care for me anymore, and don't seem to answer my prayers at all.

I haven't ever prayed for the luxuries in life. Remember years back, when I was pouring out my heart to you to heal my mom, as you did with many others while you were still on Earth? But you didn't. Yes, I had peace of mind then, but probably it was just because I learned how to accept reality and did not really experience your miracle. Remember also when I ardently prayed for a happy family? But what have I now? Thank you at least for giving me JK; he has been my inspiration since then. He's the only human being who keeps me going. He's the only human being I have learned to love. And thank you for letting me understand the depths of the father's love to his son as it was for you and Jesus.

But look at these happy families together. There are countless numbers of them in this world, and many of them don't even worship and serve you. You know how faithful I am to you. Please don't make me like Job. That's not a desirable life for believers—it's like a theatrical show for the gods of Olympus. And I believe that you're the god of life and not a god of death. But why can't you just give me a whole and happy family again? JK needs the love of a mother too. He also needs the friendship and fun of a brother or a sister. What will happen to him when I get old and he has no sibling to lean on? For years now, he's been dreaming of a brother or a sister. And I also need the love and support of a tender-hearted, loving wife.

Please forgive me, my God, I don't mean to dishonor you as the lord of my life. But I believe that you understand my struggles just as Jesus had been through all the pains we have as human beings. I pray that you understand me. I have nowhere else to go. My friends and family members have abandoned me. They are too busy enjoying life, if not coping with their challenges also. Me and JK are alone in the world. And now it seems you're leaving us too. Please heavenly Father ...

You know many times JK has asked for something from me, and although I said no at first, later I said yes. I believe you're much more than I, or any loving father on Earth. So please, I've been pleading with you to set me free from the bondage that has imprisoned me for years. Please give me a fulfilling career and a happy family.

Remember when I first accepted you, years back when I was in college? I sincerely said in my heart that all I wanted was to serve you the rest of my life. Now it seems that you have rejected me. Then when I thought I was ready for a family, I dedicated our lives to you and fervently prayed that all I wanted while serving you was a happy family. But you have allowed both my commitment to serve you and my wish to have a happy family to be broken to pieces. Those were not bad prayers. They were not materialistic wishes. They were worthy prayers. But why?

Please God, help my unbelief. At times, I think people like Leith and Elise have reason to think the way they do. I still could not let go of my faith in you because you're the only anchor in my life. JK trusts that. With me as his dad, he can make it through life every day without worry. He's not anxious about the future. Could I also be like him to you, as my heavenly father? But please show me the reasons to think so. Show me even just a hint of the miracles you have shown to others.

Please, God, you know what it means to be human. You know what it means to worry, to have broken dreams, to be left alone. I know you can sympathize with me. So please hear my cries. Just say let it be, and it will be done, as when you created the universe.

I hate to say this, and my conscience too trembles at this thought, and forgive me, but I'm losing my faith too ... I need to release the pressures in my heart; otherwise, I'll implode. Please show me a sign that you are real and you care for me. I need you to strengthen my faith, please, my God and my Savior. Strengthen my faith ... and show me the way ...

JK interrupted Krister's reflection. "Dad! Look at the birds. They must be enjoying the Falls too. Probably they're taking a shower in the mist. That's it, that's what they're doing."

Krister jerked when JK called for his attention. "Wow! That's great!" Krister said.

"Oh no! Are we going right into the Falls, Dad?" JK asked, holding firmly his dad's hands again.

"No! We're going there but we're not going to sink. C'mon, put on your raincoat hood properly, and fast," Krister said.

"Oh no!" JK let loose of his dad's hands and hugged Krister tight instead.

"That's okay! C'mon, face the Falls and I'll hold you tight." Krister slowly turned JK around to face the Falls while holding him. "See, everything is safe, everything is okay ..."

"Wow!" JK exclaimed, experiencing the Falls up close.

Before leaving the wharf, Krister looked back at the Falls as if to say to God, "Thank you, God, what next? But just hold me tight ..."

LEITH went up to the revolving Skylon Tower for the lunch buffet. He was awestruck by the grandeur of the Falls. "Wow,

that's awesome!" he said. "I could have invited Elise with me."
He gazed on the Falls for a few minutes and began reflecting ...

Where did, indeed, this grand universe came from? Of course, having a God as religion characterizes it is a nonsense notion. But what about if indeed there are the highest categories of beings that are so scientifically advanced they could create living beings from nonliving things? Could this be more probable than the big-bang? But, if supreme beings exist, where did they come from?

Elise is right. It's maddening to think about the origin of all realities. I don't need to solve this otherworldly mystery. Besides, what's the importance of this in my everyday life? Even if higher beings spawned life on Earth, they don't care about my daily life. If they did, they should have made life on Earth easier, peaceful, and equitable.

Probably, they spawned life and left it to evolve into a higher species. Some life became plants, others animals, and then human beings, the highest of all life to have evolved. But again, what about the very origin of all realities? Where did those higher beings that spawned life on Earth came from?

Oh! My goodness! This enigma is taking away my fun in Niagara. I even missed inviting Elise for a dinner.

"Man, I just missed it," he said with regrets. "Probably I'll stay for another day; perhaps I'll meet someone of the same flock."

He continued reflecting ...

Krister had seemed so sure about what he was saying about God. I still remember the silly time when I was like him. But Krister's beliefs about heaven and Earth seem to play a role in psychologically enabling him to face life with confidence. But why at times do I have an instinctive phobia about dealing with my own challenges in life? Anyway, it's not just me, it's common among all human beings.

Probably what I need is just a close friend. Or maybe it's time for me to marry. It's been a while now since I had an intimate relationship. It's like I don't even know how romance and intimacy feels anymore. I need that gentle touch, the lovely caress, the enchanting bedside talks, that enthralling physical union of two people in love with each other. Oh my! When can that happen again?

Why don't I try that online dating? Probably I might find someone who's more family-oriented and less fussier that western ladies. But how will I know if they're for real or not?

Hmm ... but why not try the church? Yeah, those fundamentalist Christian churches. You know. At least, I could be sure that with their fundamentalist and conservative way of life, they could be decent women. That could be a great idea. At least I could have more peace of mind marrying a Christian, or any religious woman, than a secular care-free woman. A religious woman has conservative values in life. And she is likely more faithful and loving to her husband than a carefree one. Or is it really ...?

But how could we have a compatible family life when I don't believe in God anymore? And she'd be going to church every Sunday, and my goodness, that would be the last place I'd like to go! Imagine the stress of sitting in the church, wasting your time, listening to a delusional 'prophet' claiming to be the spokesman of an illusory god? No, it wouldn't work! I'd enjoy loving the woman, but I'd be afflicted with a psycho-religious disease.

Why not just engage in a casual relationship with no strings attached? I'll just have fun without marital commitment. In this sense, she enjoys, I enjoy, and when it's time to part, we can bid goodbye to each other without heartache. That could be a good idea. Love, after all, is just a misnomer nowadays. It seems like love has already become obsolete. Many nowadays marry just to have companionship and support, aside from meeting each other's sexual needs. Then when they get bored with each other, they explore others more exciting than their spouses, till marriage simply breaks down. And kids suffer. Good, if both sides want a divorce; they just let go of each other. But often the innocent party is devastated. Life and careers are shattered by the wanton folly of the other partner. What an irony!

"C'mon guys!" A gleeful woman motioned to her jovial family to come. "This is where we sit. Remember, its Mom's treat this time; next it will be Dad's."

"Wow! Dad, look at the view. It's just awesome," a teen child said with excitement. Her dad peeped and said, "Okay guys let's get food first, then we'll enjoy the view while eating."

Leith's attention was caught. He continued reflecting ...

Wow! What a happy family! I think I'm just making a negative generalization about love and marriage. This family looks happy. Look at the excitement they all have. How I wish I too could have a family ... Perhaps I was engrossed laying aside religion, particularly Christianity, and have forgotten to savor happiness and contentment in life.

I rejected religion because I wanted freedom from my oppressed conscience, but it seems I'm beginning to sow pessimism in my soul too. That shouldn't be! That's not the road I'd like to travel. All I want is a happy, free life.

Happy, because I enjoy life to the fullest, despite some human imperfections. And free, because I can realize my true being without the constraints of superstitious beliefs. But how can I achieve it? Where do I start from here? I've got to start from something else ...

After pausing for few minutes, he was excited, realizing something.

That's it! That's it! I need an anchor in life, my home base where I start and come back for reference. Krister is right, and I also said it: human beings need an anchor in life ...

The Lonesome Farewell

"Well, here we are again," JK said and they laughed. "I've got to watch another movie again. I hope I won't fall asleep this time waiting for you guys."

"So what movie do you have today?" Elise asked while gently caressing JK's back.

"It's Winn Dixie," JK answered.

"Winn Dixie, as in the store?" Elise asked.

"No, it's 'Because of Winn Dixie,' and he's a dog," JK replied. "It's a cool story because people don't like each other at first be-cause they're different. But later they became friends and accept one another. And everybody's happy. I hope you guys will be friends, though you're different. Right Dad?"

"Sure, my boy!" Krister answered.

JK responded with a thumbs-up. The guys smiled, realizing again the nuggets of JK's wisdom, which they wouldn't have listened to if it were an adult telling them.

"As I promised yesterday," Elise said, "it will be my treat again. And I hope you'll remember me as well as our interesting coffee talks. I hope something good can come out of our candid conversations. I hope this rendezvous can someday help us find the answers we've all been looking for. So what shall I get for you, Krister?"

"Okay, let me try tea this time. Just any tea you can pick."

"Looks like even in drinks you're now beginning to explore alternatives," Elise said, smiling sweetly. Krister smiled too, while realizing that, indeed, he had become more open to other views on life.

"And Leith?" Elise asked.

"Okay, let me try tea as well, the Wild Sweet Orange."

"What about you, my dear JK?"

"Still the same. The yummy creamy chocolate drink."

"Looks like you guys are having tea. So why don't I try a something different?" Elise looked around. "Ah! Also the yummy creamy chocolate drink. This will make me feel younger than you guys," Elise joked. And the guys smiled.

"It looks as if we are all into the business of exploring alternatives," Leith joked back.

Moments later Elise came with the treats. "Wild Sweet Orange for you, Leith. And here's an exotic Zen tea for you, my dear Krister. And here's JK's, and this is my bottle of extra creamy chocolate drink."

"Okay, now let the ball roll for the last time," Krister butted in. JK put on his iWear and watched his movie while drinking his chocolate every now and then.

"You see, guys, I don't have all the answers to the issues you brought out against religion. But let me just point out something here. First, religion and faith in God has been a part of our way of life from education to health care, and even to national anthems throughout the world. The leading centers of education in the world have religious roots too: Harvard, Princeton, Cambridge, Oxford; as do the many leading hospitals in the world, both Catholic and Protestant. You see, religion has been the driving force behind many of our educational and health institutions, because religion provides a powerful drive in making human life better.

"And, of course, as I mentioned yesterday, religion is also an essential part of the founding of many nations. And not only Christian nations, but also those of Muslims, Hindu, Shinto, Confucians, and other religions. So what will you do with religion that is embedded in the existence of one's nation, culture, and identity? We just couldn't take these out because we couldn't rationally and concretely prove the existence of God. Imagine what would become of these countries if you took religion out. There would be chaos, identity crisis, and eventual destruction of society and people. You see, religion is not just about belief, it's about people. You take religion away, you destroy people's lives.

"Okay, say, let's take religion away, but what shall we substitute for it? Philosophy? I don't think philosophy has that deep, sublime, and sustainable driving force to shape people's lives. Something merely theoretical just passes away like a fad. A philosophy may gain people's attention for a while, but in the long run it lacks conviction and life-changing passion. There's no substitute for religion. Philosophy can't comfort one person, let alone a nation, in times of sorrow. Philosophy can't bring about the courageous spirit that religion instills.

Who shall we substitute for God? Our country? Faith in God with the spirit of patriotism? Well, in many societies patriotism is connected to faith and love of God. We just can't be rational all the time because when we face a crisis in life, reasoning just doesn't work, but faith does."

Leith smiled with a bit of sarcasm at Krister's talk.

"We need something spiritual to help and guide us in times of our deepest needs for meanings and inspirations in life. Even transcendental meditation can't provide it. All it does is provide a temporary denial of reality. But faith in God brings both serene acceptance of reality and hope beyond tragedies in life. So, if we talk about humanization, there's no better means of humanizing people than religion.

"Of course, I recognize there are undesirable fanatics in religion, but anywhere you go there are always bad apples. It doesn't mean that because we see a few rotten apples we stop eating apples. And it doesn't mean that since there are varieties of apples that we now just throw apples away without trying them to see how good they are."

Leith asked, "You mean you're also open to trying forms of religious expression other than Christianity?"

Krister was caught off-guard by the comment. "Umm … yeah! Why not? I see something good in every religion. I'll just pick up the good ones and leave the bad ones," Krister replied.

Elise asked, "So, are you moving toward a new religious synthesis? You might end up creating a new one. Not a bad idea, though, if it offers the world a fresh and synthesizing faith. Let me know someday when you find a fresh alternative to our present stale religions."

"Well, if ever I'd like to promote a new integrative religion, I'd like to start first from Christianity. Probably, an integrative Christian faith that synthesizes the good in various denominations and offers Christians a fresh and trans-sectarian Christian faith. Anyway, even if I come up with it, I foresee not having success spreading it."

"Oh? Why the pessimism? Where's your faith?" Elise asked.

"Well, you see, the Christian academe and churches are discriminative. They specify what racial voices they would hear. They don't allow contributions from other people. Just look at the leaders and thinkers of Christianity and you'll see they're racially selected. I could say the secular world is even more open to diversity and inclusion than Christians. Christians have been persistent in suppressing diversity and inclusion, particularly with ethnicity and gender. It's part of their selective outlook on faith. They always fear that when they become open they'll lose their idols and even God.

"You're right Elise, most religions are discriminative. Most Christian bureaucracies and academe are racially selective. They regard other people as less intellectual or less divine.

"You see, I have to accept that I, too, have frustrations with Christianity. It's one of the most racially segregated religions in the world. Christianity in North America, particularly the evangelical and Pentecostal forms, is nothing more than a holy, ethnic, religious spa, a place where segregated people can come every Sunday and try to make each other feel good as members of a holy band.

"I and JK, amid the challenging times in our life, have been hopping from one church to another, mainly Caucasian evangelical and Pentecostal churches. They vary from liberal to conservative. We were seeking an inclusive and welcoming church, but we found no differences among them. They were all consistent in their sectarianism and wily rejection of the contribution of what they tagged cultural minorities," Krister said, expressing his regret.

Leith said, "So, now you realize that, indeed, if God is true, he could have transformed Christians into more fair-minded people. Or at least Christian faith could have made Christians more ethnically and gender inclusive. Do Christians not believe that all people came from one couple created by God in his image?"

"I'll be honest to say that there are also important issues in my faith that I'm struggling with," Krister answered with faith amid uncertainty. "But I believe God will show me the way one day."

"Now, Krister, let me ask you this question. How do you find certainty in life?" Elise asked, sincerely, while also trying to prove Krister's ingenuity in providing faith-answers.

"My faith!" Krister answered. "I have faith in God that, although I couldn't find answers to many of my serious questions in life, he will someday—at unexpected moments —show me the way."

"Is this not a blind faith?" Elise asked.

"No. I find no such thing as blind faith. Faith believes that something you don't see and couldn't concretely figure out is possible and will be realized in a miraculous way. When we reach our limits, God intervenes when we believe in him."

"But give me something more concrete and more practical," Elise said.

"Well, when you're worried about life, leave it in God's hands. Let go of your worries, just have peace of mind and face life one day at a time. Remember that if God cares for the lilies in the field and the birds in the sky, he will also care for you. It's not about philosophical truth, it's about faith that God will perform miracles in our lives."

Hmm. I've already learned to be carefree in life. Why am I beginning to be anxious again? Elise thought.

"Well, Krister, back to the issue of synthesizing faith. Do you think that all religions are talking about the same God?" Leith asked.

"That's what I thought before. I realized, though, that each religion is talking about different Gods. God in Judaism is the one almighty Creator who has chosen Israel as his people. In Islam, he is the God who rewards faithful Muslims. The Christian God is an incarnated divine-human being and the Savior of all who become Christians. The Hindu God is an abstract God to whom everyone who is free from the cycle of birth and rebirth will eventually merge. The Shinto Gods are spirits of family ancestors. A Taoist doesn't think of God like western religions but the universal principle of existence to which we should all harmonize. Of course, Taoism also has a mixture of spirit worship. Buddhism has no God, only those who have reached enlightenment, though Buddha's image is also invoked for blessings and guidance."

"Now do you see that indeed religion is full of human-made idols?"Leith asked.

"But, you know, despite their different beliefs about God, there is still something common in it: that God does provide salvation to human beings. The important question here is not about who among the world religions has the true God, but who among them will God accept. I believe that God understands all people, and whether he will accept one form of religion over the other, it's up to him to judge, not me. What I'm concerned about is how faithful I am to him.

"But that's me. That's how I see faith. And that's what I believe. We're all different, and God deals with us in different ways. Honestly, I too have my serious struggles in life. At times, I also question God. Sometimes, I'm also uncertain of my future, despite my faith. I'm still human, you know, subject to doubts and flaws. Sometimes, I also wonder where God is. But my hope is that someday, when we meet again, we'll all be excited to share each other's discoveries in life."

"Well it looks like you're trying to bid goodbye to us now," Elise said. "I'd like to let you know that I enjoyed our conversations. And this has been helpful to me. Our coffee talks have opened my mind to some possibilities too. And I hope it's the same for you and Leith."

Leith offered to shake hands with Krister. "Thank you too, Krister. Thank you for listening to me, too." Krister shook it lightly. "And thank you, Elise." Elise raised her hand in a friendly gesture of saying you're welcome, and smiled, deciphering Leith's look. Leith then turned to Krister to continue saying something important.

"I know it's hard for you to listen to me, but you're kind enough to. You're more open-minded than many believers I know. I know most believers think of people like me as satanic or evil, but we're as sacred human beings as the religious. It's just that we found a different path in our search for meaning in life. Because we're different doesn't mean we're demonic or whatever. We also value the dignity and sacredness of human life.

"I, too, have my struggles in life. At times, I also wonder where to go. At times, I hope I could somehow get hold of something miraculous to help me make it through life. But, of course, I sense that one day I'll also find happiness and contentment. You know, that kind of life when every day you wake up, you're thankful that's it's another wonderful day, instead of dragging yourself to another challenging day. I hope I'll also find the answer I'm looking for.

Thanks again, Krister, it was a pleasure meeting you," Leith said while giving his business card to Krister, then to Elise. "And I hope you'll also explore other alternatives in your search for meaning in life, as we do. And here's my card. Let's all keep in touch."

"By the way, if you don't mind, what's your PhD in?" Krister curiously asked.

"Ironically, Theology!"

"Theology?"

"How come?"

"It's a long story. To keep it short, after teaching Theology for years, I finally arrived at the crossroad where I realized Theology is nothing but the trash of egocentric thinkers."

"Wow! And here's my card too," Elise said charmingly, handing her card to Leith, then Krister.

"May I also ask you, if you won't mind, what your PhD is in?" Krister asked.

"Anthropology. I was fascinated at how human beings developed their fine civilizations. But I ended up becoming the CEO of our property holding company when my dad passed away."

"Oh! And here's mine, as well." Krister also gave his card.

"And you also have your doctorate. And what's this?

"Doctor of Ministry."

"Now I know why you speak like a minister. So which parish are you serving?" Elise asked.

"Ironically, I resigned years ago. I could no longer accept the power play inside the church, or the skeletons hidden in the holy closets. I was also fed up with the sectarian dogmatism that separates and isolates Christians from one another. Aside from the stressing petty bickering inside the church."

"Hmm," Elise and Leith hummed at the same time.

"Well ..." Elise warmly hugged Leith, then Krister. Leith and Krister also hugged each other. At once, they realized their coffee talks had drawn them together like longtime best friends. And though they felt lonesome saying goodbye to one another, they also felt as though they all belonged to one grand mosaic of life.

Elise gently removed JK's iWear and said, "My dear, JK, I guess you still have much time left to see around."

"Oh good, it's done! Now we can go to the Bird Kingdom. Have you guys figured out what it is that you really want in life?" JK asked. "Hmm," the guys hummed in chorus, with the hunch that indeed something life-changing was about to happen in their lives.

"Let's go, Dad." JK grabbed his dad's hands, excited to go to the Bird Kingdom. While on the way out of the hotel, JK noticed something, "Dad, I saw that guy again. I also saw him yesterday. And he seemed to be listening to your conversations. I think he's up to something."

"Which guy?

"That guy?"

The guy glanced at them too.

"Never mind, let's go, Dad," JK said.

The Life-Changing Realization

*K*RISTER—

While on the Greyhound bus going back home, Krister reflected ...

"They're right. I've been harboring this pressure in my conscience for years; now it's time to let go of it ..." He took a deep breath, then slowly breathed out, as if breathing out the miasma in his soul. "At last, I'm free!" he sighed. "No more God of fear and bothered conscience. No more sectarian God. Only the God that's caring, friendly, and ever-partnering."

Then the image of Jesus tenderly holding a lost sheep flashed in his mind. "It's only you and me, my boy. It's only you and me ... but don't worry, we're not lost, and we can make it, for we have a Friend ..." he silently yet boldly said, looking at JK leaning on his shoulder, sleeping. Then he hummed the song, *What a friend we have in Jesus* ...

296

LEITH—

On the plane back home, while gazing at the sky, Leith reflected …

You're right, Krister. I came to enlighten you, but you enlightened me instead.

Yes, I need an anchor in life … but it couldn't be an anchor in the gods of religions though. No, not a mystical anchor but, yes, still a relational one … Yes, it's the anchor based on fulfilling human relationship—family—the family that loves, cares, and supports one another. And also relationships with my friends. I need to nurture and enrich these relationships. These are my anchors in finding fulfillment in life.

Well, it looks like it's time to make phone calls and visit people I've dearly missed for so long.

But most of them are believers, and how do I fit it? I'm sure, in time, they will learn to accept who I am …"

Leith smiled anticipating his future.

ELISE—

Elise, on the night before leaving Niagara, sat in a lounging chair in her hotel room overlooking the magnificently lit Falls. While watching in awe, she began thinking …

297

You're right Krister, I need to let go of the pressures within me. I needed time to meditate and have peace with my soul. Yeah! Now I get it! Meditation! But what kind of meditation? Hmm ... not the meditation of conscious focusing. Not the meditation of conscious emptying ...

But that's it—the meditation of harmonious life with the universe. But no, not just meditation—a way of life.

Now, no more philosophical answers and endless confusion, but a daily harmonious life with nature and my fellow human beings. Could it be that this is what I've been seeking? Wow, I'm on my new journey in life ...

She was excited.

THE JOURNALIST—

Laying on his bed and staring at the ceiling, he reflected ...

They all spoke sense. If only they could blend their views, they could create a breakthrough, a fresh worldview. But if I were to blend it, what would it be ...?

Hmm ...

Yes! That's it! And that's who I am! I am a believer who thinks there could be the originator of reality because reality must have a beginning. If there are different beings on

Earth—humans and animals—different beings of animal species from microbes, worms, clams, fish, ants, monkeys to dolphins—there could also be different beings in the universe. And there could also be the universal Supreme Being.

But the nature of that being is not human. And its reality is beyond the human world. The God religion created is very human and clannish, nothing but an idol. So I am also an atheist who does not believe in worshiping an exclusive portrayal of the originator of realities. Because the reality that originated all realities could not be limited to exclusive religious personification. In human terms, we may call it the Supreme Being, but its nature is beyond human understanding. So I'm also an agnostic who understands that nothing final can be said of the originator of all realities.

But what will I substitute with religion and God?

That's it!

He was excited.

"Um!" He jerked when the doorbell rang, stood, and opened the door.

"Dad!" His excited eight-year-old son hugged him, followed by his six-year-old daughter. He hugged and kissed them too.

"Honey!" His wife hugged and sweetly kissed him.

"Dad, how did your snooping go?" his son asked.

"Well, interesting, shocking, mind boggling, but stimulating!"

"But honey, what happened here? The room is messy. And look at yourself, you look like a weirdo with a beardo."

"Are you a Santa Claus, Dad?" his daughter asked.

His wife laughed, and so did he.

"Tell me what happened to you, Hon."

"Well, I've been trying to solve the mystery."

"Like Nancy Drew, Dad?" his daughter asked?

They laughed again.

"Well, Hon, you can't stretch yourself trying to solve the mystery. Mystery will just unfold itself every day. C'mon, have yourself a bath, dress up and shave yourself. I'd like to see the suave guy in you. Honey?"

He smiled, seeing his wife's charm while envisioning something very life-transforming and fresh ...

*There's more to a butterfly's life
than crawling as a worm.*

FreshIdeasBooks

An avenue for the unheard voices
to freely express their creative thoughts.

FreshIdeasBooks offers a one-stop
(print, eBook, audio book)
publishing opportunity!

www.FreshIdeasBooks.com

About the Author

lan J. Delotavo, PhD, uniquely fuses candid theological critiques and profound life experiences in his writing. As a former theologian and minister, he thought he knew the depths of faith. However, it was his years spent taking a life-changing journey along the ragged edges of life that transformed him into a new person with a fresh perspective on faith and human life. Out of confusion he found new revelations. Out of brokenness he found new life.

He hopes that his books inspire the development of a grander, more liberating and empowering faith beyond the confinements of controlling sectarian traditions. He is passionate about writing books that refresh our outlook on faith and guide us toward more creative and fulfilling lives.

Visit his Web site at www.delotavo.com.